novum pro

Eva Fogarasi Bálint

FAITH, SCIENCE AND THE SUPERNATURAL
The Missing Jigsaws of Christianity

novum pro

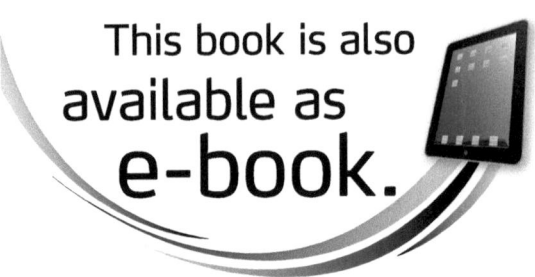

www.novum-publishing.co.uk

All rights of distribution, including via film, radio, and television, photomechanical reproduction, audio storage media, electronic data storage media, and the reprinting of portions of text, are reserved.	© 2018 novum publishing ISBN 978-3-99064-360-0 Editing: Rachel Begley Cover photo: Jaturon Ruaysoongnern | Dreamstime.com Cover design, layout & typesetting: novum publishing
Printed in the European Union on environmentally friendly, chlorine- and acid-free paper.	**www.novum-publishing.co.uk**

This book is dedicated to all
who wish to reflect upon
the visible and invisible reality

———————————

Boundless gratitude to Per Anglert
for all the support and good advice

CONTENTS

INTRODUCTION 9
   Unusual Visit 9

QUARKS AND PHOTONS 13

"WHAT IS TRUTH?" 17

JESUS' TEACHING ABOUT THE UNIVERSE 22

BILOCATION AND
OUT-OF-BODY EXPERIENCES 30

THE PHYSICAL BODY IS
ONLY A "GARMENT" 36

IT IS THE SPIRIT WHO GIVES LIFE 39

THE DUAL NATURE OF JESUS CHRIST 49

JOURNEY TO OTHER DIMENSIONS 54

NEAR-DEATH EXPERIENCES 64

HUMANS 74

WHAT JESUS TEACHES
ABOUT THE CREATION 82

"THE ENLIGHTENED INSIGHT" 90

EVE'S THIRST FOR KNOWLEDGE 94

SPIRITUAL KNOWLEDGE 98

IS OUR "CHIMPANZEE BRAIN" ABLE TO
CREATE AND STORE THOUGHTS? 103

PADRE PIO AND "THE BOOK OF LIFE" 110

THE SUPREME BEING IS THE
ONE GENERATOR OF ALL
RADIANCE AND VIBRATION 119

COLLECTIVE EXPERIENCE
OF PARANORMAL PHENOMENA 131
   Madonna Apparitions in Fatima and Zeitoun 131

THE MULTITUDE OF GODS 140

"WHO DO THE CROWDS
SAY THAT I AM?" (Luke 9:18) 149

DID JESUS DIE ON THE CROSS? 170
   Before Crucifixion 170
   The Crucifixion 172
   The Empty Tomb 177
   Jesus Meets the Disciples After the Crucifixion 180

"WHO HAS BEWITCHED YOU?"
(Galatians 3:1) 193

"I WAS BLIND, BUT NOW I SEE" 204

LITERATURE AND SOURCES 208

INTRODUCTION

Unusual Visit

While I was busy preparing dinner in the kitchen, my daughters, Kinga and Réka, were in full swing with a lively play in the living room. They were jumping on the couch, were running around the desk and then through the glazed veranda they ran back to their room.

After warning them to be careful, I went back to the kitchen hoping that none of them gets hurt while running around. Kinga was five years old and Réka is a year younger.

Suddenly it became completely silent inside. My first thought was that some of them had fallen and got hurt, so I rushed to check what had happened.

To my greatest surprise both girls were on their knees in the veranda and were staring at the large window overlooking the courtyard. *"We saw Jesus,"* Kinga said when I asked what they were doing. *"He looked in and smiled. But he quickly disappeared."*

The girls were taken by this experience but they did not understand the depth of what had happened. However, I began to examine the incident in my mind. I knew that no physical human being could "look in" through the veranda window and disappear quickly as we lived on the second floor. The veranda window faced the courtyard and the gate was always locked, so nobody could climb high up, look in and disappear in a second. Neither could the girls' vision be a fantasy production as it happened in the middle of a pretty wild game. They were busy with running around and not with imaging that Jesus should look in through the window.

When I tried to discuss the girls' experience with my family and some of my friends they laughed embarrassed and made skeptical comments. Their reaction and attitude did not surprise me as the whole society and the people's belief and life was influenced by the communist materialist thinking. "God does not exist, religion is opium for the people" was the doctrine everybody had to learn and believe in. Especially during dictator Ceausescu's time there were hard prohibitions against everything that had to do with religion. Teachers and persons with managerial functions should not participate in religious ceremonies and no literature with religious content could be sold in bookshops. As we belonged to the Hungarian minority in Transylvania, we got to live with the constant threat that our churches would be closed down or demolished. Only the Rumanian Orthodox Church, which was considered to be cultural heritage, was approved by the state. The only religious book we had in our home was a Bible and a prayer book which I had smuggled in from Hungary at a time when we were on holiday there. I got spiritual inspiration and support from sister Miriam, a former Roman Catholic nun who became "civil" when the monastery she used to live in was closed down and the nuns were chased away by the communists.

Later I have asked my daughters several times to tell me about their vision and even today, after more than thirty five years they describe the event with the same words as they did when it happened. Their story is very simple: "Jesus looked in, he smiled and then he disappeared".

At that time I had no idea about religion -psychology which I later studied at the University of Lund in Sweden, where I learned that a good method of reviewing a supernatural experience was to let the person tell the story again and again and that if the experience was real than the "story" will be exactly the same. I did not know either that quantum physics and the scientists' research of subatomic particles could help me to understand the miracles of Jesus, my daughters' vision and the experiences that I had in adolescence and later on in life.

During my theological studies and later as a priest in the Swedish church I realized that supernatural phenomena do not fit in the restrictive theological framework of the institutional Christianity. Biblical science and rigid dogmas stand in the center when teaching and talking about God and belief. Christianity has become the religion of the Book – The Bible and not of experiencing God. Martin Luther, John Calvin and other theologians of Reformation mistrusted religious experiences. They put the word, The Bible and preaching at the center.

The situation got not better in the 1900s when the German theologian Rudolf Bultmann (1884–1976) intended to promote Christianity by declaring that "wonder stories" in the Bible had a mythological character and that they should be interpreted only symbolically. Bultmann believed that the world is governed by natural laws and therefore wonders and miracles which exceed the laws of the universe, have no place in a modern interpretation of the world. He rejects miracles as real events by saying that they do not fit the laws of the universe.

Several prominent scientists of modern times, as Max Planck, Niels Bohr and Albert Einstein, argue, contrary to Bultmann, that the universe is much more sophisticated than one previously thought and that a full explanation of reality is perhaps impossible based only on the laws of nature and physical theories they know.

Christian theologians and the clergy have tried to "amputate" people's spiritual beliefs and thinking by claiming that the only truth of God can be found in the Bible and the dogmas formulated by the institutional church.

After many conversations with Christians in Sweden and other European countries, I have come to the conclusion that many people question some of the strange dogmas of their religion. They are confused because of the contradictory image of God as found in the Old Testament and The New Testament, as well as of questions like:
- is The Old Testament really a holy book, even though it contains stories about Moses, Joshua, David and other religious leaders who encourage genocide and war in the name of God?
- can God be loving and merciful but cruel and punitive at the same time?
- do people really inherit sin already when being born?
- could God not forgive sins without sacrificing his son on the cross?
- if Jesus died for our sins, why should he judge the living and the dead at the end of times?
- is it right to believe in paranormal phenomena that the institutional church rejects?
- is faith compatible with science?

To contemplate these questions is much easier than giving a final answer to them.

While I was searching for the missing jigsaws of Christianity, I was surprised to find that there are many similarities between Jesus teaching about the spheres and the life beyond and what mediums and people with paranormal abilities report, as well as what scientists assert about the visible and invisible reality.

QUARKS AND PHOTONS

As the mysteries of the universe as well as of the origin of Earth and humanity has always fascinated man, scientists, philosophers and theologians have tried to answer the big existential questions concerning matter, spirit and other visible and invisible jigsaws of the reality we are confronted with.

Man attempted to explore the smallest components of matter already about 400 years before Christ when Greek philosophers and scientists maintained that atoms are indivisible components of nature and of universe. Later physicists realized that the atom is divisible and actually consists of particles such as electrons, protons and neutrons. These elementary particles were considered to be the tiniest components of the Universe.

Today physicists know that even that theory was wrong as the atom is made up of smaller particles than protons and neutrons. They research the mysteries of the subatomic particles which, according to several scientists, may not even be considered as matter in the word's real sense, but it is more like a "spirit-matter".

The atom was thought to be similar to a solar system in miniature whose components spin and circle with a mechanical precision. But in 1920 when a huge particle accelerator was built in Switzerland and nuclear physicists started to chase after subatomic particles of the matter, they realized that *the atomic world is full of darkness and chaos.*

Scientists, with Albert Einstein and the Danish physicist Niels Bohr at the head wondered if the atom is a real thing or it is only an abstract creation of human mind.

Those subatomic particles that the scientists have discovered, are called leptons, mesons, peonies, baryons, quarks, photons, and even "God's particle.

But what is a quark and what is a photon? **Paul Davies,** a well-known nuclear physicist, writes in his book *God and the New Physics,* that quarks are assumed to be *"genuine, structureless elementary particles"* which, like many other subatomic particles, are "invisible" as they are hiding and never *"show themselves."* Paul Davies concludes that *none of the subatomic particles, whether quarks or some others, are considered to be particles in the ordinary sense. In fact, they might not even be matter.*

The exact description of the structure of matter the physicists do are only advanced mathematical abstractions according to Paul Davies.

Nuclear physicists define subatomic particles as a "quantum" – a quantity of something. There are only speculations and assumptions about what that "something" could be. The physicists realize that the way they have so far perceived nature, matter and the universe is no longer enough. They admit that approximately ninety-five percent of the universe consists of invisible, unknown matter which they call "dark matter".

Many scientists think that a comprehensive understanding of the laws of nature and of the universe is actually beyond the rational thinking.

"The only thing we do know is that what we think today will be a thing of the past tomorrow" writes the nuclear physicist Gary Zukav in his book *The Dancing WO-LI Masters.* However, despite shortcomings and limitations, quantum mechanics help nuclear physicists to research the subatomic particles of matter, may they be visible or invisible. They have discovered, for example, that subatomic particles act after *decisions taken elsewhere.*

This 'elsewhere' can be as far away as in another galaxy! Scientists also say that subatomic particles can be in two places at the same time, that is they "bilocate".

Can this interesting discovery be a start for scientific explanation of supernatural phenomena? Will scientists soon prove that powers belonging to an unknown, invisible reality may influence the decisions and actions in our physical world? Jesus maintains that he comes from another world (sphere) and that the words he speaks and the works he does are not on his own authority, but the Father who dwells in him does the works. May his statement be interpreted that all he did and said was decided and controlled elsewhere?

The Master says to the disciples who sometimes are confused about his words and identity:

*"Do you not believe that I am in the Father, and the Father in me? The words that I speak to you **I do not speak on my own authority;** but the Father who dwells in me does the works." (John 14:10)*

Supernatural phenomena such as telepathy, bilocation (to be present in two locations at the same time), Jesus' unexplainable acts and peoples' supernatural revelations have been rejected by scientists as phantasmagoria. They forget that there had been many scientific theories which at first were suspected to be "phantasmagoria", but later they proved to be correct.

At the same time we know that neither supernatural nor scientific explanations are always reliable and that some of them really are fabrications.

Nuclear physicists in Switzerland keep on hunting for a particular subatomic particle that should give the final answer about BIG BANG and other mysteries of the visible and invisible reality. Champagne bottles were opened and Nobel prize was awarded when nuclear physicists working at CERN stated that a new subatomic particle, later called Higg's particle, was for a very short moment "seen" on the computer screens. Even if the physicists are not sure that the "thing" they saw on the computer screen was a real particle with mass or only an energy field, professor Higg, leader of the project, believes that the phantom figure on the screen could have been the missing jigsaw for giving answer on all the enigma of the universe. Does this sound credible? When professor Higg was asked by a journalist, what happens if their new discovery will be proved to be wrong, he answered that in that case they would "hit upon" something else.

More than two thousand years ago Jesus surprised the Jews, the scribes and even Pilate when saying:
"You belong down here, I am from above. You belong to this world, I do not belong to this world ... I am who I am and I do not do anything of myself, but speak as the Father has taught me "(John 8:23 ...)

When Pilate wants to get more information about the Master, whom the Jews wanted to be condemned to death, Jesus said to him:
"My kingdom is not of this world. *If My kingdom were of this world, my servants would fight, so that I should not be delivered to the Jews; but now my kingdom is not from here ... I was born, and for this cause I have come into the world, that I should bear witness to the truth. Everyone who is of the truth hears My voice.*
Pilate said to Him: **What is truth?**"*(John 18:33 ...)*

"WHAT IS TRUTH?"

If we want to understand the mystery of Jesus, we have to start with finding out what he meant when saying *"My kingdom is not of this world"*.

Jesus often spoke of an invisible "realm"/dimension which he called the Kingdom of Heaven, the Kingdom of God or The Realm of the One including the universe, our planet as well as everything existing within and outside us, uniting in a fascinating way the visible and invisible reality.

When talking to the crowds about the Kingdom of God, he used parables and words that everyone could easily understand. He said: *"the Kingdom of Heaven is like **leaven,** which a woman took and hid in three measures of meal till it was all leavened' "(Matthew 13:33)*

*"The kingdom of heaven is like **a mustard seed** which a man took and sowed in his field. It is the smallest of all seeds, but when it is grown it is greater than herbs and becomes a tree, so that the birds of the air come and nests in its branches. "(Matthew 13:31)*

Jesus brilliantly puts the microcosmic elements of mustard seed and of the invisible leaven in a larger, macro-cosmic context – that of the WHOLE. His "scientific" method differs from that of the modern nuclear physicists' who, while chasing the subatomic particles of the matter-universe, miss the knowledge and the truth about the Whole Universe that includes not only the visible but also the invisible reality that actually cannot be researched in laboratories or particle accelerators.

Jesus' purpose was to supply his closest disciples with knowledge – *gnosis* about the mysteries of the universe. This is very evident in the scriptures that were found by accident in December 1945 by Muhammad 'Ali al-Samman and his brother in Upper Egypt in the neighbourhood of Nag Hammadi. The brothers had no idea that they made a very valuable archaeological discovery while digging sabakh, a loose soil they used to fertilize their crops with. It just happened that they ran into a jar of clay. First they thought the jar may contain a *jinni, a spirit* or gold, but, when they smashed it, to their great disappointment, they only found old books, bound in leather.

When the brothers went home, they told their mother to use the books to light the fire, so some of them were burned up.
 A few weeks later, Muhammad Ali and his brother revenged their father's death by murdering Ahmed Ismail. As they knew that the police would investigate the murder, they asked the priest of the village to store the papyrus books that had not been burned up. Maybe they intended to sell them later. Both the priest and the history teacher of the village realized that the books had a great value.

The scriptures were then sold to antique dealers in Cairo and later, after many adventures, ended up in the Coptic Museum in Cairo. After many difficulties and circumstances researchers got access to the very valuable fifty-two texts which now are called *Nag Hammadi Scriptures*.

Researchers are not sure concerning the dating of the original scriptures, but it is much evidence that some of the texts, or parts of them, circulated from Galilee to Rome and Greece to Asia Minor, even before the year 100 AD. *The Secret Book of James, The Secret Book of John, The Gospel of Philip, The Wisdom of Jesus Christ, The Dialogue with the Savior, The First Revelation of James, The Second Revelation of James, The Letter of Peter to Philip, The Gospel of Mary and The Gospel of Judas-* seem to include texts written by disciples soon after the crucifixion of Jesus.

According *The Secret Book of James,* "*The twelve disciples were all sitting together, recalling what the Savior had said to each of them, whether in a hidden or an open manner, and organizing it in books. I was writing what is in (my book)."* *(The Secret Book of James: 2.7)*

The so called gnostic books were probably used of a Christian group called gnostic.
    Gnosticism was not a religion with a distinctive cult and organization like Judaism, Christianity, Zoroastrianism, and other mystery religions.
    Gnosis means *knowledge* gained *through insight* and personal experience and involves a process of seeking knowledge about oneself, about God and the universe.

In order to answer the question why these scriptures have been hidden for more than 1500 years, we have to recall that there were **disputes and struggles between the institutional orthodox church, later called Catholic, and the gnostics.** The authorities of the new established institutional church were intolerant against other Christian groups and their teachings and claimed exclusive legitimacy. They decided that only the so called canonized (authorized) scriptures should be valid and used in the rites. In the Easter letter of 367, Athanasius, Bishop of Alexandria, gave a list of the twenty-seven books of The New Testament that should be canonized (authorized).

When Bishop Athanasius wrote the Easter letter that had to be read in all the monasteries of Egypt, he called upon to eliminate all other books that he called "illegitimate and secret". It was around this time that monks, or a monk living in St Pachomius monastery put the books into a big jar that was buried not far from Nag Hammadi.

The precise dates of the composition of the fifty-two tractates in the collection of Nag Hammadi codices are uncertain, but, according to researchers, most of them are from the second and third centuries CE. It is supposed that they were originally written in Greek and translated into Coptic. However, some books – gospels – contain material, texts that maybe originate directly from Jesus's nearest disciples.

The authorities of the institutional Church were keen to prohibit these scripture because the gnostic gospels present totally different information about God, the One as well as about Jesus and his doctrines.

The gnostics rejected worshiping the God of Israel who, according to their opinion reigns as a king and lord, is a mere craftsman, or an avenging judge who gives the law and judges those who violate it.

The doctrine of God and the religion questions discussed in the different groups also involved social and political issues, especially when 1 Clement, Bishop of Rome (c 90-100) argues that the God of Israel alone rules all things; he is the lord and master whom all must obey; he is the judge who lays down the law, punishing rebels and rewarding the obedient. Clement writes in a letter addressed to the Chorinthians that God delegates his "authority of reign" to "rulers and leaders on earth" who are the bishops, priests and deacons. Whoever refuses to "bow the neck" and obey the church leaders is guilty of insubordination against the divine master himself. Whoever disobeys the divinely ordained authorities "receive the death penalty".

One generation later Ignatius of Antioch in Syria defended the same principle, but he went further than Clement. He claimed that, as there is only one God in heaven, there can be only one bishop in the church; "the laity" had to revere, honor, and obey the bishop as he was the representative of God.

The gnostic Christians criticized the development of church hierarchy. Instead of ranking their members into superior and inferior "orders", they followed the principle of strict equality. When they met, all the members, men and women participated in drawing lots in order to designate who should take the role of priest, to offer sacrament, read the scripts or to address the group as a prophet. The next time the group met, they would throw lots again, so that the persons taking each role changed continually.

According to the gnostics and several scripts found in Nag Hammadi, **the mission of Jesus on Earth was not to save mankind from sin through a bloody sacrifice on the cross but to teach spiritual insight and to give** *gnosis* – **knowledge about the spheres of the universe as well as about the spiritual origin of humans.**

JESUS' TEACHING ABOUT THE UNIVERSE

Jesus purpose was to turn the heart and thoughts of the Jews from the image of God according to the Old Testament to the Supreme Celestial Being of uni/multiverse whom he calls The One. According to several gnostic texts, Jesus said that the creator described in The Old Testament is not the Supreme Being of the universe, but is a lesser divine being who created copies of the original glorious creation of the One. His assertion that The One Supreme Celestial Being is different from the God of Israel upset the scribes, the Pharisees and the chief priests with whom the Master often argued about the image of God, and because they were not open for new knowledge. He even admonished them with sharp words:

"*But woe to you, scribes and Pharisees, hypocrites! For you shut up the kingdom of heaven against men; for you neither go in yourselves, nor do you allow those who are entering to go in;*" (Matthew 23:13 ... 34)

According to *The Wisdom of Jesus Christ* as well as other Nag Hammadi texts, Jesus presented the Supreme Divine Being as the primal Source which appears as a "dyad", as Father-Mother. The Primal Father is Ineffable and eternal and the Primal Mother is Insight, Grace, Silence, the Womb and "Mother of All". He talked about these things to the disciples who" *were confused about the true nature of the universe, and the plan of salvation, and the divine forethought, and the strength of the authorities, and everything the Savior was doing with them in the secret plan of salvation.*"

"*The Savior said to them, 'I want you to know that all people born on earth from the foundation of the world until now are of dust, and though they have inquired about God, who he is and what he is like, they have not found him. The wisest of people have speculated on the basis of the order and movement of the universe, yet their speculation has missed the truth. It is said that philosophers voice three distinct opinions about the order of the universe, and they disagree with each other. Some of them say that the world governs itself, others say that divine forethought governs it, still others that fate is in charge. All these opinions are wrong. Of the three opinions I have just mentioned, none of them comes close to the truth. They are mere human opinions.*

I have come from infinite light; I am here, and I can tell you exactly what the truth is.'" (NH Scriptures: The Wisdom of Jesus Christ 90,14 …)

Mathew said to him, *"Master, no one can find truth except through you. Teach us the truth.*

The Savior said, "**The One Who Is is ineffable**. *From the foundation of the world until now, no power, no authority, no creature, no nature has known the One Who Is.*

Only the One Who Is, and anyone to whom this One wishes to give revelation through the emissary from the first light, knows the One Who is. Henceforth, I am the great Savior.

The One Who Is *is*
immortal and eternal, *and being eternal, is without birth,*
for whoever is born will die;
unconceived, without a beginning,
for whoever has a beginning has an end;
undominated, **without a name,**
for whoever has a name has been made by another;
unnamable, with **no human form,**
for whoever has a human form has been made by another.
The One Who Is has an appearance of its own,
not like anything you have seen and received,

*but an alien appearance that surpasses everything
and **is superior to the universe**.
It looks everywhere and beholds itself in itself.*

*The One is infinite,
incomprehensible,
and constantly imperishable ... ...
and is called the Father of all.
(NH Scriptures: The Wisdom of Jesus Christ 93,24 ...)*

The disciples listen, but they do not always understand the cosmology Jesus presents. He talks about his passing spheres when he traveled to our planet and he says that he feared to be detected by the evil ruler of the world, the "jealous god" called Yaldabaoth who wanted to catch him. Jesus says that he had to change shape during his journey to our planet.

*"**I traveled in the realm of great darkness**, and continued until I entered the midst of the prison. The foundations of chaos shook, and I hid from them because of their evil, and they did not recognize me.*

*Again I returned, a second time, and went on. **I have come from the inhabitants of light** ...*

... ...

Again, a third time, I went forth –

... ...

***I am the light dwelling in light** ...*

I brightened my face with light from the consummation of their realm and entered the midst of their prison, which is the prison of the body." (NH, The Secret Book of John, Hymn of the Savior, 30,11 ... 31,25)

It is astonishing that people who had near-death experience, also talk about darkness that they had to pass when they were ascending to the Realm of Light.

Betty J. Eadie, who had a near-death experience, reports in her book *Embraced by the Light* how she felt when she traveled through the darkness:

> "When you are in the presence of enormous energy, you know it. A deep rumbling, rushing sound began to fill the room. I sensed the power behind it …
>
> **Darkness** began to surround my being …
>
> I felt as if I had been swallowed up by an enormous tornado …
>
> The darkness was more than a lack of light; it was a dense blackness unlike anything I had known before … within this black mass I felt a profoundly pleasant sense of wellbeing and calmness. I felt myself moving forward through it, and the whirling sound became fainter …
>
> The speed became so incredible that I felt that light years could not measure it …
>
> I became aware of other people as well as animals traveling with me, but at a distance. (page 35 … 38)

Betty recounts that the black mass took the shape of a tunnel through which she traveled "at an even greater speed, rushing toward the light."

Jesus knew that it was not enough only to talk about the mysteries of the universe, but it was also important that the audience in general and some of the closest disciples in particular should witness and experience the dual nature of the visible and invisible reality. Sometimes he taught them by letting them to experience his dual nature, the spiritual and the physical one.

John and James experienced for example that Jesus' body was sometimes hard as a rock and another time completely soft. Even if they knew about Jesus' dual nature and his paranormal abilities, the disciples were amazed and sometimes scared when experiencing that the Master "changed shape".

> "When I was at the table he let me lie in his bosom, and I leaned against him. And **sometimes felt his chest weak and soft but sometimes hard as stone,** so that I marveled, saying 'How can it be? ' …
>
> Another time he took me along with James and Peter up on the mountain where he used to pray, and **we saw in him such a light** that a

person who uses a common language cannot possibly describe what it was like. He took us three up on the mountain, and said:

'Come with me!' And we went …

I approached him gently so that he could not see me, and I stood there and looked at his back. And I saw that he had no garment on (the author's interpretation: no garment means no physical body) *but I saw him naked* (as a spirit)*, and he was not at all like a man. His feet were whiter than snow, so that even the ground lit up by his feet, and his head reached to heaven. And I was appalled and cried to. But when he turned around, he appeared to be like a little man, and he took hold of my beard, pulled at it and said: 'John, be not faithless, but believe. And be not so curious.'*

And I said to him, ' Lord, what have I done?' And I tell you, brethren, that in that place, where he pulled me by the beard, I felt such pain for thirty days that I said to him, ' Lord, if the little pulling of my beard when you were joking with me, hurt so much, how it would have felt if you hit me!' And he said to me:' You should not tempt the one who cannot be tempted.' …

I will tell you of another oddity, brothers. When I wanted to touch him, I felt a solid and firm body. But sometimes, when I touched him, the body was immaterial as a spirit, yes, as if it did not exist." (The Apocrypha of John)

A similar experience is recorded in a Nag Hammadi script, *The Second Revelation of James* in which we read that James, Jesus stepbrother once embraced the Master and did not find him as he thought he would be.

Jesus said to James, "*'My beloved! Look, I shall reveal to you what the heavens have not known, nor their rulers. Look, I shall reveal to you what that one did not know – the one who boasted … … I am alive … Don't I have (power) over everything? Look, I shall reveal (to you) all things. My beloved, understand and know these things, (that) you may come forth from this body and be as I am. Look, I shall reveal to you what (is hidden). Reach out your (hand) and embrace me.'*

At once I reached out my (hands), but I did not find him as I thought he would be. After this I heard him say, 'Understand, and embrace me.'

*Then I understood, and I was afraid, yet I rejoiced with great joy."
(Nag Hammadi Scriptures, The Second Revelation of James 56,14, page 338 ... 339)*

Skeptics doubt such stories classifying them as "tales" and say that the experience of John and James contradicts the laws of nature. Nobody can be hard as a stone one moment and soft like a sponge next moment! However, taking into account that 70% of the human physical body is water that can be hard as ice, "soft" as liquid and "immaterial" as steam depending of the temperature, the energy it is exposed to, the phenomenon is not totally impossible. Scientists know that the texture of the matter can be converted by changing the vibrations and frequency of the matter-particles. We cannot prove, but only suppose that Jesus knew a lot about the laws of the visible and invisible reality as well as about the vibrations and frequencies of matter of different densities and that is why he was able to do works that amazed and astonished people.

Theologians have been arguing about the nature of Jesus Christ several times during the history of Christianity. Those who do not want to accept Jesus' divine origin claim that he was only a mortal man with prophetic ambitions. There are Christians who want to see in him only a celestial being, a divinity whose body was a substitute.

Another phenomenon that puzzled the disciples was Jesus'ability to appear suddenly passing closed doors. According to the *Gospel of John*, the Master appeared after the crucifixion first to Mary Magdalene, who was weeping in despair at his empty tomb.

Nobody knows in what shape Jesus appeared to Mary at the tomb, but, taking into account his dual nature and his knowledge about the laws of the visible and invisible reality, his apparition could have been a bilocation for instance. As there are several texts in the New Testament reporting that Jesus suddenly appeared to the disciples who were sitting behind bolted doors, it is supposed that Jesus had the ability to bilocate similarly to Padre Pio, an Italian monk who was the greatest mystic of the 19th century.

Actually, all over the world there are uncountable stories which report about people experiencing an "unexpected visit", despite closed doors, of relatives or friends who had passed away. People who had out-of-body or a near-death experience also say that walls or locked doors do not prevent a spirit-entity to move anywhere in space.

The disciples who had listened several times to Jesus' discourses about the universe, about the visible and the invisible reality, were scared every time when they were confronted with the Master's double nature, the physical and the spiritual one. They certainly believed in his paranormal abilities but never understood the mystery behind them. They did not realize that Jesus probably took advantage of the relativity of space and time when passing the "borders" of the different dimensions of uni/multiverse. He was able to change the vibration frequency of his matter-body every time when moving between the visible and invisible world.

According to Einstein space and time are not separated but they form a unit that he calls space-time which actually is relative. Two thousand years before Einstein, Jesus also talked about the relativity of time and space when saying to the disciples:

"If you consider how long the world has existed before you and how long it will exist after you, you will see that your life is but a day and your sufferings but an hour."
(NH Scriptures, The Secret Book of James 4,22)

As a priest in the Swedish Church, I have listened to many people who had experienced that a deceased person, a spouse, a mother or father had payed a visit to them not in dream, but "in reality". Other people wanted to speak about a paranormal experience that was more real for them than anything else in their life even if they were not able to explain it logically.

Experiencing the supernatural is not easy. At first one is scared, shaken and overwhelmed and then one is filled with joy but sometimes also with skepticism. "Can it be true? Am I crazy? How could it happen? Is there any scientific explanation? Can *teleportation* be a scientific explanation of the out-of-body phenomena? Was Jesus teleported from one dimension to another? Was he really able to bilocate?", are questions that people have in the mind.

Research of the *teleportation of subatomic particles* is already going on. Some scientists say that in the remote future it may happen that people will not take the plane when traveling from New York to Paris, but they will be "teleported". This sounds like science-fiction, just as people considered the first airplanes and later the first spaceships to be. In the 18th century people in Asia, Africa or Europe could not even dream of the possibility of watching and listening "live" to the president of America while he is talking in Washington. Today this is the most natural "phenomenon" that people experience when watching TV.

BILOCATION AND OUT-OF-BODY EXPERIENCES

Bilocation is a phenomenon that has both perplexed and fascinated people. How can a person who lives on one continent appear and be seen on another continent without having left his living place? According to scientists this is impossible and they consider the phenomenon to be pure fantasy. But for people who have experienced that a person who lived far away suddenly appeared to them, bilocation is a very real occurrence.

How supernatural experiences are interpreted depends on the view of life one has got. Most of scientists doubt paranormal abilities. On the other hand, people who have a dualistic view of life regard bilocation and other paranormal experiences as signs proving the existence of a reality beyond our visible matter world.

Numerous witnesses in different religious traditions have reported about bilocation. In modern time P**adre Pio,** an Italian monk who during 50 years was living in the monastery of San Giovanni Rotondo, had the charisma of bilocation. There are several documented testimonials from different countries according to which friar Pio appeared suddenly to people in America, Hungary, Uruguay and other countries. He was seen in different places in Italy too where everybody knew that actually he never left the monastery of San Giovanni Rotondo.

In 1951 father Pio appeared unexpectedly and celebrated Holy Mass on a convent of nuns in Czechoslovakia. After Mass, the nuns went to the sacristy to offer Padre Pio coffee and to thank him for his unexpected visit, but they did not find him in the sacristy and no one had seen him being there at all. Thus the nuns realized that his presence at the Mass was thanks to his bilocation ability.

In 1956, during the revolution in Hungary, Cardinal Mindszenty was arrested and put into jail where, to his surprise, he got a very special visitor. It was Padre Pio who appeared in the cell of the prison, talked to him and celebrated Holy Mass with him. When later Cardinal Mindszenty reported of this remarkable visit, everybody knew that Padre Pio never paid a visit to Hungary, so his presence in the jail had another explanation.

Don Orione, a Catholic priest was very surprised to see Padre Pio at a Mass in Rome, as he knew that by that time the friar was not allowed to leave the monastery in San Giovanni Rotondo.
"I was in Saint Peter's Church in Rome in order to attend the celebration of Saint Teresa's beatification," don Orione reported later. *"Father Pio was there too, despite the fact that he was in his convent at the same time. I saw him. He was smiling and coming towards me through the crowd, but when he was not far from me, he disappeared."*
Even the pope was informed about the event, but after a short investigation they had to realize that Padre Pio had not violated the convent rules according to which he was not allowed to leave the monastery without getting the permission of his superiors. He could be seen in Rome while he physically was in San Giovanni Rotondo thanks to his bilocation ability.

On the 20th September 1918 Padre Pio received *Jesus' wounds on the cross – the stigmata.* When his superiors heard what had happened, they decided to keep quiet and avoid publicity concerning the unusual phenomenon. Padre Pio was not allowed to leave the monastery and for several years he was not allowed to celebrate Mass in the church of the monastery. But the report about the monk with the bleeding stigmas was circulating in Italy and even in other countries, and aroused the curiosity of scientists and medical experts. As the Vatican was afraid of scandal, doctors were called to examine the wounds on friar

Pio's hands, feet and side. Physicians could not give any logical explanation why the continuously bleeding wounds never inflamed and why one could feel a peculiarly fragrant aroma of the blood from the wounds.

Bilocation was not the only ability padre Pio had. He heard voices, experienced visions, healed people and as a medium could predict events that later proved to be true.

One of padre Pio's dearest friends was the physician dr. Sanguinetti. On the evening of January 20, 1936 dr. Sanguinetti and two other laymen were visiting padre Pio in his room. Suddenly padre Pio knelt down and asked them to pray "for a soul that is soon to appear before the tribunal of God." They all knelt down and prayed. When they arose padre Pio asked them: "Do you know for whom you prayed? ... It was for the King of England."

When hearing this dr. Sanguinetti was surprised, as the local papers had reported that the king was suffering only of the flu and he was in no danger. Padre Pio felt a little uncomfortable with their doubt, so he said shortly: "It is as I say" and then he changed the subject.

Next day in the afternoon the Italian newspapers announced the death of George V, King of England.

Padre Pio was never interested in analyzing or giving an explanation to his "supernatural" abilities. When he was asked about his ability of bilocation, the closest "scientific" explanation he ever gave was when he said that it occurred *"by an extension of the personality"*.

"Dr. Sanguinetti asked padre Pio about this charismatic phenomenon:
 – Padre, the doctor said, when God sends a saint elsewhere by bilocation, is he aware of it when that occurs?
 – Yes. One moment he is here and the next moment where God wants him to be.
 – But is he really in two places at once?

– *Yes.*
– *But how is that possible?*
– *Through an extension of the personality,"* said Padre Pio.

When a confrere insisted to get an explanation to his bilocation ability, father Pio said: *"Ask God and not me whether it's true or not that I am experiencing bilocation, trilocation or whatever. All I can tell you is that I always try to do His will. For this reason, I am always where I am."*

Another time he said: *"If Christ could multiply the loaves and fishes, why should he not be able to multiply me?"*

How this "multiplication" could occur is so far a mystery. Friars living in the same monastery experienced many times that when Padre Pio was "traveling", that is he was bilocated, his body was rigid and he seemed to be total unconscious of people who physically were near to him. Father Alberto, who 1917 met Padre Pio, reported:

"I saw Padre Pio standing in front of the window, looking at the mountain. He was speaking to himself. I approached him in order to kiss his hand, but he did not notice my presence and I noticed that his hand was rigid. At the same time I heard him clearly giving absolution and pardon to someone.

After a while Padre Pio shook like awakening from a nap. He looked at me and said: 'You are here. I did not realize it!'

A few days later a telegram from Turin was delivered. Someone thanked the superior of the convent for having sent Padre Pio to Turin to assist a dying person. I realized that the man was dying in the same moment I heard Padre Pio blessing and giving absolution to a for me 'invisible' person when I entered his room in San Giovanni Rotondo. Obviously, the superior of the convent had not sent Padre Pio to Turin. He had bilocated there."

When the brothers living in the monastery asked if the people who owned this remarkable ability were aware of "moving" to a different place, Padre Pio said: *"Of course, they know about it. They do not know whether it is the body or the soul that moves, but they are fully aware of what is happening and where they travel. "(Ulrika Ljungman, page 115)*

Pilots of different nationalities (British, Americans, Polish, Palestinians) and with different religious background (Catholics, Orthodox, Protestants, Jews, Muslims) who were stationed in the south of Italy during World War II were perplexed when they saw "a monk in the heaven," who prevented them from dropping bombs on German installations close to San Giovanni Rotondo.

General Bernardo Rossini did not believe the pilots' report about the monk "flying in the sky". As the pilots failed their task, the General decided to lead the attack against a German weapons depot.

The General and the crew took off, heavily equipped. When they approached the target and would let the bombs fall, "the mysterious monk" with raised hands appeared in the sky. The crew and the General did not care about him, they wanted to fulfill the attack, when the bombs they were releasing did not detonate and the aircraft they were sitting in changed course without the pilot steering it, the crew and the General gave up the attack.

When the war was over, the General and some of the pilots traveled to San Giovanni Rotondo where the General met padre Pio and identified him as "the monk in the sky". It is said that padre Pio put his hand on the General's shoulder and said with a smile: "Oh, it was you who wanted to bomb out all of us!". (Renzo Allegri, *I miracoli di Padre Pio*)

The General fell to his knees and then became one of Padre Pio's spiritual children.

How could it happen? Was it a hallucination or a dream? I had these questions in my mind when Padre Pio had appeared at my bed one morning when I was fourteen. I did not see his whole body or the bleeding wounds, but only his face. He was looking at me with a kind and warm smile and then disappeared very quickly. Sister Miriam, a Catholic nun who gave me private lessons in German at that time, had told me about Padre Pio and his wounds, but as my family is protestant, I was confused concerning the belief in supernatural phenomena. I was a teenager who liked Elvis' music and danced rock and roll, but at the same time I liked going to Mass with sister Miriam whom I admired for her spirituality.

When I told my mother about my strange experience, she thought that it was a dream as she had not the slightest idea of who Padre Pio was. When sister Miriam heard about my "vision", she doubted not that my experience was real as she knew about padre Pio's bilocation ability.

THE PHYSICAL BODY IS ONLY A "GARMENT"

According to gnostic scriptures, Jesus had many interesting dialogues with his nearest disciples about the human nature. He said that the spirit, the soul, the mind and consciousness inhabit the physical body which is only a perishable garment. He encouraged the disciples to know themselves pointing out the divine origin as well as the double nature of humans. He talked about the difference between the spirit (Greek: *pneuma)* and the soul (Greek: *psyche)* and said that **soul is** actually **the captured spirit in the body**. He said:

"He (the Father) knows about desire and what flesh needs. Does it not desire the soul? The body does not sin apart from the soul just as the soul is not saved apart from the spirit. But if the soul is saved from evil and the spirit too is saved, the body becomes sinless. ***The spirit animates the soul but the body kills it*** *..."* (*The Secret Book of James, 11,30)*

Jesus talked about *the One, Invisible, Imperishable and Pure Spirit* that animates all the living in the invisible and visible realms. He called the Invisible One Spirit for *Light* and said that he himself came from this Light.

"The One is the Invisible Spirit. We should not think of it as a god or like a god. For it is greater than a god, because it has nothing over it and no lord above it ...

The One is immeasurable light, pure, holy, immaculate" (NH, *The Secret Book of John, 2,25 ... , page 108)*

According to the Nag Hammadi scriptures, The Master said that the *feminine life-giving power* called Hawah (Eva) or even Barbelo, came forward from the Light similarly the Father. The feminine life-giving entity is the first revelation of the One Who Is, and she is the womb of all life in universe.

"*His (*The One's*) thought became a reality, and she who appeared in his presence in shining light came forth.* **She is the first power** *who preceded everything and came forth from his mind as the Forethought of the All.* **Her light shines like the Father's light; she, the perfect power, is the image of the Perfect and Invisible Virgin Spirit** ...

She became **the universal womb,** *for she precedes everything,"* (NH, The Secret Book of John, 4,19 ... 6,10)

When Jesus explained the spiritual origin of man, he talked about the descendancy and the ascendency of the humans, as well as about "the imprisonment" of the spirit in the physical body.

The creation in the spiritual sphere was perfect until a deity called *Sophia* (means *Wisdom* in Greek) took a bad decision: she wanted to create something by herself without the consent of the Invisible, Pure and Imperishable Spirit. The result of Sophia's creation is a half-god and half-demonic creature, called Yaldabaoth, the child of the chaos, who soon starts creating own realms with archons and angels.

According to Nag Hammadi texts the human race is created by Yaldabaoth and his archons who at first were able to produce only a robot that could neither raise up nor walk. As the chief-creator, Yaldabaoth is desperate when realizing this, the archons suggest him to blow the spirit of his mother Sophia into the face of the "the robot-body". Yaldabaoth follows their instruction without knowing that his mother's spirit actually was the Spirit of the Imperishable One, the Supreme Power of All. Yaldabaoth is very surprised and jealous when the robot-body, after getting the spirit, is more intelligent and shines more brightly than he, the creator and the co-workers, the archons. As they feel threatened, they decide to hide this bright image of the first human in a physical body formed of clay. So, the good news is that we, humans are actually deities who have inherited high spiritual abilities which are "hidden" in the clay-body.

Jesus was aware of the difficulties of living an undefiled and pure life in the matter-body which is continuously subjected to temptations coming from negative energies of lower spheres. He knew that his disciples needed to be filled with the good and positive energies of the Light in order to fight against "the robbers", that is the demonic powers of Yaldabaoth, the jealous creator. As he knew that humans generally are ignorant about all these things, he exhorted his disciples to learn themselves in order to understand the truth about their double nature, the spiritual and the physical one, as well as about the WHOLE, the Universe.

IT IS THE SPIRIT WHO GIVES LIFE

The people Jesus spoke to, including some of the disciples, were not able to understand His teaching about the invisible spiritual dimension from which he had come. The visible body of flesh and blood was the only reality they could easily understand and relate to, as flesh and blood was an important part of the religious cult of the Jews. In Jerusalem the temple priests sacrificed thousands of animals- and not so long before even men. As the Jews believed in a punitive god who punished Israel when committing sins, they thought that the blood of sacrificed animals appeased the wrath of Israel's God. Jesus criticized the Jews' way of thinking of God and wanted to change their opinion by turning their attention from the visible sacrifice cult to the invisible, spiritual aspect of reality. In order to convince them, the Master used parables that later are misunderstood and misinterpreted by gospel authors, Christian theologians and priests. Jesus saying, **"I am the living bread"** is such a parable which the author of the Gospel of John, or a later Bible editor interprets in a specific way. We read:

'I am the living bread which came down from heaven. Whoever eats of this bread will live forever. The bread I will give is my flesh, which I shall give for the life of the world'

The Jews therefore quarreled among themselves, saying, 'How can this man give us his flesh to eat'

Then Jesus said to them, 'Most assuredly, I say to you, unless you eat the flesh of the Son of Man and drink His blood, you have no life in you.' (John 6:51 …)

According to the gospel, the Jews are upset and the disciples are astonished when hearing this; some of them leave, so they do not hear what Jesus explains concerning the parable.

"When Jesus knew in Himself that the disciples complained about this, He said to them, 'Does this offend you?'
It is the Spirit who gives life; the flesh profits nothing. The words that I speak to you are spirit, and they are life. *"* (John 6:62–63)

It is doubtful that Jesus encouraged his disciples and followers "to eat his flesh and drink his blood" while he was alive. It is more probably that the author of the text, or later editors have put together different sayings of Jesus making an own interpretation of them. Actually, we do not read this story in any other scripts.

It is very improbable that Jesus, who was against all kind of sacrifice cult, should suddenly encourage people to "eat his flesh" and "drink his blood". There are no other books or texts, except those in the New Testament, suggesting that Jesus intended to introduce an "eat my flesh, drink my blood" ritual.

One should also recall that spreading false and contradictory rumors about Jesus and his teaching has always been the purpose of some groups who never could accept him. To assert that Jesus had encouraged his followers to eat his flesh and drink his blood was certainly a good way to discourage Jews from converting to Christianity.

It is noteworthy that the first Christians did not practice any special rites. When they came together, they ate together the food they had taken from home, they prayed together and recalled what Jesus said and worked.

The authors of the gnostic gospels do not mention anything about Jesus having admonished the disciples to eat his flesh and drink his blood. As the phrase "eat my flesh and drink my blood" occurs only in the scripts of the New Testament, we suspect that it was Paul together with some early church fathers who started propagating this strange idea. As a former Pharisee, called Saul, he knew that the cult of sacrificing animals in the temple of Jerusalem was a compulsory tradition that fulfilled the rules of the Old Testament. According to the book of *Ezekiel* a lamb should be offered every morning on the altar of the temple. We read:

"You shall daily make a burnt offering to the Lord of a lamb of the first year without blemish; you shall prepare it every morning." (Ezekiel 46:13)

Paul wants to "reform" this pagan tradition of the Jews by saying that Jesus is the Lamb of God who has been sacrificed for the sins of men. It was not anymore necessary to sacrifice animals every morning as the blood of Jesus has reconciled God with the world for ever.

Paul did not realize that he propagated a pagan image of God when talking about Jesus as the Lamb of God who is sacrificed for our sins.

Jesus would have never accused The One, Who Is Light and Love, for causing pain to and killing him. According to John 16:2, he said to some of his closest disciples that those who thought that they offered God service when they killed a person, did not know the Father and Jesus at all:

"They will exclude you from the synagogues; yes, the time is coming when **those who kill you think they offer God service**.

And these things they will do **because they have not known the Father nor Me.**" *(John 16:2)*

Christian theologians assert that Jesus did not only accept but he even looked forward to be sacrificed for the sins of mankind. But Jesus' prayer, **'Father, forgive them, for they do not know what they do.'" (Luke 23:33 … 34),** as well as his declaration **"woe to that man by whom the Son of Man is betrayed! It would have been good for that man if he had not been born." (Matthew**

26:24), contradict the theologians' assertion that Jesus considered the crucifixion to be the fulfillment of God's will. When the chief priests, the solders of the temple, and the elders came to arrest him, Jesus said to them: *"this is your hour, and the power of darkness."* (Luke 22:52) This declaration of Jesus makes evident that the crucifixion was the will of the power of darkness.

After the destruction of the Jerusalem temple in 70 AD, the Jews "reformed" their religion and stopped sacrificing animals. Christian priests on the other hand go on, even today, with sacrificing Jesus as the Lamb of God when celebrating Mass. According to the Italian monk Padre Pio, Jesus does not appreciate the priests' offering him in Mass. Jesus talked about this in a vision which the friar had one morning; Padre Pio recounts the apparition of Jesus in a letter addressed to Friar Augustine on April 7, 1913.

'My dear father,

I was still in bed on Friday morning, when Jesus appeared to me. He was tormented and his face and body expressed pain. He showed me a great crowd of priests, even ecclesiastical dignitaries. Some of them were celebrating Mass, others were putting on or taking off their Mass vestments.

I was very sad when I saw pain on Jesus' face. I asked him why he suffered so much. He did not answer. He turned his face away and looked at the priests, but shortly after he seemed to be horrified and he turned his face from them. I saw tears on his cheeks.

Jesus left the crowd of priests and expressing disgust on his face, he cried: '**Butchers!**'

Then He told me: 'My child, do not think that my agony has been only the three hours on the cross, no; actually, because of the souls I love, my agony will be going on forever. My child, while I am agonizing, you should not fall asleep.

My soul is longing for some pity, but they are indifferent and leave me alone ... (The world of Padre Pio 3 – page 168)

Jesus told Padre Pio more things that the friar should keep secret.

Padre Pio was surely chocked of Jesus's calling the Catholic priests "Butchers". Presumably this revelation and dialogue with Jesus had great impact on the friar's opinion of the Holy Communion.

When Padre Pio was asked what the Holy Communion meant to him, he said:

"***It is a sacred participation in the passion of Jesus.*** *All that the Lord suffered in His passion, I suffer, to the extent that it is possible to a human being. And that is apart from any merit of mine, but entirely due to His goodness.*"

"I die mystically at the Holy Communion. The Communion is the culminating point of my suffering."

"**My Communion is a union**. Like the candles that fuse together and cannot be distinguished one from the other."

"**The Eucharist gives an idea of the union we will have in heaven.**"

"The offertory is the moment when the soul becomes detached from all that is profane."

"**Mass is redemption of your soul** and reconciliation with God."

"I want to save my soul at any cost."

"If it depended on me I would never leave the altar."

Padre Pio maintained that he was not alone at the altar during Mass; there were many celestial beings who attended him. *"The Angels attend my Mass in legions,"*, *"The angels around the altar adore and love," "The Holy Virgin assists me,"* he used to say when talking about Mass.

People taking part in the Mass celebrated by the friar, said that it was obvious that Padre Pio was not "alone" at the altar. It was also known that, although he never used to preach, his Holy Communion lasted at least one hour. His superiors asked him to respect the rules and reduce this time to half an hour, but this was very difficult for Padre Pio. Finally he had to surrender and follow the rules of the Church.

*"My heart beats fast when **I am with Jesus in His blessed sacrament**. Sometimes it feels like it wants to jump out of my chest. **At the altar I feel sometimes that my entire being is glowing** ",* Padre Pio said to a person who often took part in the Mass.

*"How Gentle the Spirit of Jesus is! I get confused and I only want to cry and repeat: **Jesus, the bread of life, my soul's nourishment!**",* he said another time. *(Ulrika Ljungman: Padre Pio of Pietralcina, page 62)*

It should be noticed that Padre Pio does not say that Mass is "a sacrificing Jesus- ritual" that appeals to God, but he says that it is a "sacred participation in the passion of Jesus". He does not either talk about eating Jesus' flesh and drinking his blood, but he points the "Gentle Spirit of Jesus" to be the bread of life and the nourishment of the soul. He also says that the Communion is a spiritual union with Jesus.

Besides Padre Pio there are many other people who experienced the "real" presence of Jesus Christ when taking part in the Holy Communion.

Gunnar Hillerdal and Berndt Gustafsson, Swedish theology professors, are authors of a book titled: *They saw and heard Jesus* in which they report about people who saw Jesus to be present when the priest was distributing bread and wine in the Holy Communion.

A woman, who wished to remain anonymous when the authors published her story, tells the experience she had when taking part in the Holy Communion in the little church of Onsala 1966 or 1967:

"My experience is just as clear to me as the day it happened," wrote the woman, who that Sunday had to go alone to church as her man was ill. She wanted to attend the service, but she did not feel for taking part in the Holy Communion. While she was thinking *"Next time I will do it",* suddenly she saw that a very strong light appeared at the end of the pew she was sitting on. She could not see any figure in the light, but she heard clearly somebody saying one word: *"Christ".* Then she heard the voice saying: *"One who does not eat **with me**, cannot be a part of me."*

After hearing these words, the woman went in a hurry to the Communion table; she realized that nobody else in the church noticed anything of what she had seen and heard.

The woman was surprised to hear the expression "***with me***", as she was not sure if one can find this in the Bible. She was used to hear the priest saying that one should "eat" Christ's body and "drink" his blood, but this voice ***invited her to eat with Christ.***

The woman did not tell about her experience to anybody; she kept it in her heart as a "sweet secret". Later, when she wrote her letter reporting the revelation, she confessed: *"We are cowards as we do not dare to bear witness to Christ. We do not dare to confess that he is among us."* (G. Hillerdal/B. Gustafsson, page 27–28)

A man, born 1920, writes about a vision he got in a church when attending his son's confirmation:

"It happened in the Church of Snötorp where I took part in a confirmation sermon as my son was a candidate. When it was time for the Holy Communion I fell on my knees at the alter rails where suddenly in front of me appeared in a light a man with shining white clothes, with his arms slightly outstretched to me, just like he wanted to embrace me. My body started to shake.

Even if my experience was very real for me, I have told about it only to few people." (Hillerdal, page 32, – document 13 1973)

An 80 years old woman sent the following report (document 31) to professor Hillerdal:

"This happened in a small country church in Värmland many years ago, in 1946. As it was Holy Thursday evening, the priest, who had prepared the holy sacraments, invited us to the Communion table.

When my husband and me were standing there to take the sacramental bread and wine, I got an astonishing vision that was a very big thing in the life of such a little human being as I consider myself to be.

The priest 'disappeared' and instead of him a beautiful and very shiny figure was standing there ..." (Hillerdal, page 32)

It is noteworthy that people reporting their special experience while taking part in the Holy Communion, do not mention anything about Jesus "the Lamb" offered on the altars, or about his "flesh and blood" presence in the bread and wine. They recount instead about a "beautiful and very shiny figure" being present at the Holy Communion.

Once I myself experienced the presence of Jesus Christ at a Communion in the Baptist Church in Haywards Heath in England.

I was on a visit at my daughter and her family; on Sunday I went to Church with them. When it was time for the Holy Communion, the congregation stood up and sang a beautiful hymn accompanied by an orchestra. As I wanted to sing with them I concentrated on the big screen showing the text.

All of a sudden my attention was drawn on a very special vision: *I saw Jesus rejoicing and dancing around.* He wore a long white robe and was moving about half a meter above the floor and beamed of joy.

The vision did not last long but it made a strong impression on me. My whole body was filled with warmth and I got tears in my eyes. "He is here, he is here!" I whispered.

Theologians and church leaders, bishops and popes have many times argued about the meaning of the Eucharist. **The simple meal the first Christians shared** when they gathered for prayer, has later become a complicated ritual that finally has led to quarrels and schisms of the Christians.

The early established institutional church, later called *Catholic* (that means in Greek **universal**) wanted to maintain its exclusive right of celebrating Mass. They assert even today that only Catholic priests, bishops and the Pope have got the "exclusive right" to bless and give thanks for the sacramental bread and wine which, according to their faith, is transformed into Christ's flesh and blood in the very moment the celebrant raises the chalice and pâté and reads the Eucharist prayer. This "magical" transformation is called *transsubstantiation* which means that the substance of the bread and the wine offered is really changed. According to dogmas of the Catholic Church *"The signs of bread and wine become, in a way surpassing understanding, the Body and Blood of Christ."* The outward appearance of the bread and wine, that is accessible to the senses, remains unchanged.

The doctrine of transsubtantiation according to the Fourth Council of the Lateran in 1215 says: *"His body and blood are truly contained in the sacrament of the altar under the forms of bread and wine, the bread and wine having been transubstantiated by God's power into his body and blood."*

In October 1551, the Council of Trent confirmed the doctrine of transubtantiation and defined it as *"that wonderful and singular conversion of the whole substance of the bread into the Body, and of the whole substance of the wine into the Blood – the species only of the bread and wine remaining …"*

According to the rules of the church, the bread and wine that has become flesh and blood is allowed to be distributed only to those Catholics who have confessed themselves, and absolutely not to the Christians who do not belong to the Catholic Church.

During the Protestant Reformation, the doctrine of transsubstantiation became a matter of much controversy.
Jean Calvin, the reformer did not believe in the "magical powers" of the Catholic priests. He neither believed in any kind

of substantial transformation of the bread and wine, but he **believed in Jesus' invisible, spiritual presence during the Holy Communion**. He considered the bread and wine as visible symbols of the spirit of Christ and he believed in a "spiritual feeding".

Martin Luther, who was originally a Catholic priest and monk, is more careful when defining what the meaning of the Holy Communion is. He believes that the bread and wine remain fully bread and fully wine while also being truly the body and blood of Jesus Christ. He says that within the Eucharistic celebration the body and blood of Jesus Christ are objectively present "in, with, and under the forms" and he calls it Real Presence.

In England, **Archbishop John Tillotson** decried the *"real barbarousness of this Sacrament and Rite of our Religion"*, considering it a great impiety **to believe that people who attend Holy Communion** *"verily eat and drink the natural flesh and blood of Christ. And what can any man do more unworthily towards a Friend? How can he possibly use him more barbarously, than to feast upon his living flesh and blood?"* (Discourse against Transubstantiation, London 1684, 35)

Anglicans generally consider no teaching binding concerning the Holy Communion. Some Anglicans, especially Anglo-Catholics and some other High Church Anglicans accept transubstantiation while others do not. Official writings of the churches of the Anglican Communion have upheld belief in the Real Presence. Some recent Anglican writers speak of an "objective presence" of Christ in the Eucharist indicating the possibility to believe in transubstantiation but at the same time they do not limit once belief only to it.

Theologians and priests writing dogmas about Jesus' flesh and blood offered in the Holy Communion, seem to have missed the Master's teaching that "It is the Spirit who gives life, the flesh profits nothing." (John 6:63)

THE DUAL NATURE OF JESUS CHRIST

The dual (two) nature of Jesus Christ has always been disputed. Some have claimed that Jesus was an exceptionally gifted man but not God. Others say that he is God, and that only his appearance was human. The crucial mistake of the theologians and clergy is that they do not make difference between Jesus, the divine being coming from the Eternal Light, and God, The One Supreme Being of universe.

The Church Council that met in Chalcedon in AD 451, has produced the following statements of Jesus' dual nature:
"Our Lord Jesus Christ is one and the same God, perfect in divinity, and perfect in humanity, true God and true Human ...

Christ, Son, Lord, Only-begotten, manifested in two natures without any confusion, change, division or separations.

The union does not destroy the difference of the two natures, but on the contrary the properties of each are kept, and both are joined in one person." (Justo L. Gonzalez, "The Story of Christianity", vol.1, Harper San Francisco 1984)

The statement of the Church Council that Jesus is "God" is surprising as there are no scripts confirming that Jesus considered himself to be "true God". When he presented himself as a divine being, he said that he has come from the Light and that he was the light. The disciples experienced his double nature, i.e. the divine and the human one, but they never considered him to be "true God". When the Master talked them about God, The One Supreme Being, they did not identify him to be that Supreme Being. Jesus and the disciples prayed to the

Heavenly Father. Paul, the Apostle prayed "in the name" of and "through" Jesus Christ:

… …
I call upon you,
you who exist and preexisted,
in the name exalted above every name,
through Jesus Christ,
King of the eternal realms.
Give me your gifts, with o regret,
through the Son of Humanity,
the Spirit,
the Advocate of truth.
Give me authority, I ask of you (The Nag Hammadi Scriptures: The Prayer of the Apostle Paul, page 17)

Before the crucifixion Peter, the disciple had seen Jesus in a vision as a figure of light intertwined with Holy Spirit. We read in The Revelation of Peter, found in Nag Hammadi,

"*I saw him apparently being arrested by them. I said, 'What do I see, Lord? Is it really you they are seizing? And who is the one smiling and laughing above the cross? Is it someone else whose feet and hands they are hammering?'*

The Savior said to me, **'The one you see smiling and laughing above the cross is the living Jesus.** *The one whose hands and feet they are driving nails is his fleshly part, the substitute for him. They are putting to shame the one who came into being in the likeness of the living Jesus. Look at him and look at me.'*

When I looked, I said, 'Lord, no one sees you. Let's get out of here.' …

Then I saw someone about to approach us who looked like the one laughing above the cross, but this one was intertwined with holy spirit, and he was the Savior. And there was an unspeakably bright light surrounding them and a multitude of ineffable and invisible angels praising them." *(Nag Hammadi: The Revelation of Peter, 81,3 … 83,15)*

Jesus tried hard to help the nearest disciples to understand how his double nature worked. When he meets his stepbrother after the crucifixion and James says that he was troubled when he heard what the Jews had done with the Master, Jesus comforts him by saying that he never did suffer and never was distressed and that those people did not harm him. Guess how perplexed James was when hearing this! Probably, Jesus intention was not only to give him comfort but also to point out his double nature.

We read about James' meeting Jesus after crucifixion and their dialogue in *The First Revelation of James:*

"They were waiting for the sign of his coming, and it came after some days. James was walking on the mountain called Gaugela (perhaps Golgatha – in Syriac, Gagultha), *along with his disciples, who still listened to him with desire. They had a comforter, and they said, 'This is the second teacher.'*

The crowd dispersed, but James remained behind and prayed ..., as was his custom.

The master appeared to him. He stopped praying, embraced him, and kissed him and said, **'Master, I have found you. I heard of the sufferings you endured**, *and I was greatly troubled. You know my compassion. Because of this I wished, as I reflected upon it, that I would never see these people again. They must be judged for what they have done, for what they have done is not right.'*

The master said, *'James,* **do not be concerned for me** *or these people.* **I am the one who is within me. Never did I suffer at all, and I was not distressed. These people did not harm me.** *Rather, all this was inflicted upon a figure of the rulers, and it was fitting that this figure should be destroyed by them.'"* (Nag Hammadi: The First Revelation of James, 30,16 ...)

Jesus' statement that he did not suffer and was not distressed when he was crucified is a surprising information as the institutional Church has based its central dogma on Christ' sacrifice and suffering. As the Master's physical body, "the garment" had been badly tortured, hi surely suffered lack of oxygen which caused his losing consciousness maybe the moment his physical suffering increased This was interpreted that he was dead, but actually there are several evidences that he was not clinically dead, he only fainted on the cross.

Jesus' statement "Never did I suffer at all" is easier to understand if we listen to people reporting a near-death experience. They also assert that they did not feel any pain when, because of a car accident or very serious illness, their spirit left their physical body for a while.

Raymond A. Moody, a well-known researcher on the subject, collected and systematized thousands of reports of near-death experience. In his book *Light In The Tunnel,* we read the story of a kid he calls Jason, who also says that he felt well while having a near-death experience.

Jason was eleven years old when he got a bike for his birthday. The next day, when he went out to ride the bike, he did not see a car coming on the road, so the accident was inevitable.

Jason remembered later the moment the car hit him. He said that he was outside his body and could see that it was bleeding and lying under the bike. He saw that his leg was broken and his eyes were closed. He experienced that he was floating above his body and then above the ambulance that came to collect him. He saw from above the people who were standing there and were worrying. As he felt good, he wondered why they were so worried. *"I tried to tell them that **I am well,** but no one of them could hear what I said".*

Jason also reported about the tunnel he passed through and the bright light shining at the end of the tunnel. He said that two men accompanied him during his journey through the tunnel.

When he had left the tunnel and was in the light, he could see many unknown people around. He felt their love and happiness.

"I think the light was God", Jason commented later. *"When I was in the light, I did not want to return to my body. I almost had forgotten about it"*, he said.

The two men, who were on his side all the time, told him that he had to turn back to his life on the earth. *"I went back through the tunnel and found myself in the hospital,"* Jason said.

Two doctors were working hard to rescue the boy's life. When Jason regained consciousness, he tried to tell his near-death experience, but neither the doctors nor his mother seemed to be interested to listen to or to believe his story. When he went back to school, he told the schoolteacher about his experience and the teacher contacted Raymond A. Moody, the researcher.

If we suppose that also Jesus had a near-dead experience on the cross, then we can conclude that he too, similarly Jason, did not feel any pain or distress because his spirit left his collapsed body.

Jason recounts that he tried to tell his near-death experience to the doctor and to his mother, but they were not so much interested in listening to him.

Dr *Eben Alexander,* a neurosurgeon and professor at the medical faculty of Harvard University, author of the book *Proof of Heaven – A Neurosurgeon's Journey into the Afterlife,* confirms that doctors are not interested in listening to patients who wish to talk about a near-death experience. He also started reading about the phenomenon only after having experienced itself.

"As a neurosurgeon, I'd heard many stories over the years of people who had strange experiences, usually after suffering cardiac arrest: stories of traveling to mysterious, wonderful landscapes; of talking to dead relatives – even of meeting God Himself.

Wonderful stuff, no question. But all of it, in my opinion, was pure fantasy ... Or so I would have told you before my own brain crashed.

During my coma my brain wasn't working improperly – it wasn't working **at all**. *(Proof of Heaven, page 8–9)*

JOURNEY TO OTHER DIMENSIONS

On 10th November 2008 *Dr Eben Alexander* got bacterial meningitis, a disease that strikes out the most central functions of the brain. First the cortex, where the memory, the speaking ability, the emotions and the logical thinking is coordinated, was knocked out totally, then the very dangerous bacterial inflammation spread even to the spinal fluid and deeper structures of the brain.

Dr Eben Alexander was basically "brain dead" during the days he was in a coma.

About 10 percent of the people, who get bacterial meningitis, survive the disease, but, because of the brain damage they have got, they do not have any chance to live a normal life anymore. They live a vegetative, inactive life.

To the surprise of all the doctors, who had treated Dr Eben Alexander, he did not only survive the mortal disease, but he even totally recovered later. However, this was not the only surprise. His colleagues were absolutely astonished when, after recovering, doc Alexander said that during his coma he had experienced a universe that was more real than the one we live in during our life on the earth.

"While I was in coma my brain hadn't been working improperly. It hadn't been working at all. *The part of my brain that years of medical school had taught me was responsible for creating the world I lived and moved in and for taking the raw data that came in through my senses and fashioning*

it into a meaningful universe: that part of my brain was down, and out. And yet despite all of this, I had been alive, and aware, truly aware, in a universe characterized above all by love, consciousness, and reality …

What I'd experienced was more real than the house I sat in …" (Proof of Heaven, page 129–130)

Before the disease Dr Eben Alexander was skeptical about all the stories of supernatural experiences, but the days in the coma has changed his views. During his near-death experience he got insight into other dimensions where he received a lot of valuable information and knowledge of the human mind, spirit and soul as well as about a reality that is more real than that which we experience in our physical world.

"We have been seduced into thinking that the scientific world view is fast approaching a Theory of Everything (or TOE), which would not seem to leave much room for our soul, or spirit, or for Heaven, and God. My journey deep into coma, outside of this lowly physical realm and into the loftiest dwelling place of the almighty Creator, revealed the indescribably immense chasm between our human knowledge and the awe-inspiring realm of God.

There is nothing about the physics of the material world (quarks, electrons, photons, atoms, etc.), and specifically the intricate structure of the brain, that gives the slightest clue as to the mechanism of consciousness." (page 154)

"For all of the successes of Western civilization, the world has paid a dear price in terms of the most crucial component of existence – our human spirit. The shadow side of high technology – modern warfare and thoughtless homicide and suicide, urban blight, ecological mayhem, cataclysmic climate change, polarization of economic resources – is bad enough. Much worse, our focus on exponential progress in science and technology has left many of us relatively bereft in the realm of meaning and joy, and of knowing how our lives fit into the grand scheme of existence for all eternity.

Questions concerning the soul and afterlife, reincarnation, God, and Heaven proved difficult to answer through conventional scientific means, which implied that they might not exist. Likewise, extended consciousness phenomena, such as remote viewing, extrasensory perception, psychokinesis, clairvoyance, telepathy, and precognition, have seemed stubbornly resistant to comprehend through 'standard' scientific investigations. Before my coma, I doubted their veracity, mainly because I had never experienced them at a deep level, and because they could not be readily explained by my simplistic scientific view of the world." (Prof of Heaven, page 152–153)

Eben Alexander writes about his traveling between different spheres of the universe. First he came to a realm where he experienced darkness and discomfort and where language, emotions and logic were all gone: *"these were all gone, as if I had regressed back to some state of being from the very beginnings of life, as far back, perhaps, as the primitive bacteria that, unbeknownst to me, had taken over my brain and shut it down."* (page 29)

Soon he left this dark, uncomfortable place and he came to **the realm of light**.
 "Something had appeared in the darkness.
 *Turning slowly, it radiated fine filaments of **white-gold light**, and as it did so the darkness around me began to splinter and break apart.*

Then I heard a new sound: a living sound, like the richest, most complex, most beautiful piece of music you've ever heard …

The light got closer and closer, *spinning around and around and generating those filaments of pure white light …*
 Then, at the very center of the light, something else appeared … An opening. I was no longer looking at the spinning light at all, but through it.

The moment I understood this, I began to move up. Fast. There was a whooshing sound, and in a flash I went through the opening and found myself in a completely new world. The strangest, most beautiful world I'd ever seen.

Brilliant, vibrant, ecstatic, stunning ... I could heap on one adjective after another to describe what this world looked and felt like, but they'd all fall short. I felt like I was being born. Not reborn, or born again. Just ... born.

I don't know how long, exactly, I flew along. (Time in this place was different from the simple linear time we experience on earth..) But at some point, I realized that I wasn't alone up there.

Someone was next to me: a beautiful girl with high cheekbones and deep blue eyes." (page 38 ... 40)

Dr Eben Alexander finds out later that the beautiful girl he was traveling with, was his biological sister, whom he had never met during his earthly life, as he grew up with adoptive parents and did not have any contact with his biological siblings. This sister was young when she died.

The girl communicated with him without using words.

"The message had three parts," relates dr Eben, *"and if I had to translate them into earthly language, I'd say they ran something like this:*

'You are loved and cherished, dearly, forever.'

'You have nothing to fear.'

'There is nothing you can do wrong.'

'We will show you many things here', the girl said, ... 'But eventually, you will go back.'

To this, I had only one question.

Back where?

Remember who's talking to you right now. I'm not a soft-headed sentimentalist. I know what death looks like. I know what it feels like to have a living person, whom you spoke to and joked with in better days, become a lifeless object on an operating table after you've struggled for hours to keep the machine of their body working. I know what suffering looks like, and the grief on the faces of loved ones who have lost someone they never dreamed they could lose. I know my biology, and while I'm not a physicist, I'm no slouch at that, either. I know the difference between fantasy and reality, and **I know that the experience I'm struggling** *to give you the vaguest, most completely unsatisfactory picture of, **was the single most real experience of my life.**"* (page 40 … 41)

Eben Alexander felt that a *divine breeze* changed everything in that world, shifting everything into a higher octave, *a higher vibration*. There was a divine being behind or within this celestial breeze, so he started putting questions wordlessly.

Where is this place?
Who am I?
Why am I here?

Each time I silently posed one of these questions, the answer came instantly in an explosion of light, color, love, and beauty that blew through me like a crashing wave … Thoughts entered me directly. But it wasn't thought like we experience on earth … These thoughts were solid and immediate … and as I received them I was able to instantly and effortlessly understand concepts that would have taken me years to fully grasp in my earthly life."(page 46)

Although Eben Alexander would have liked to stay forever in that beautiful world, he was happy to be back in his earthly life and be again together with the people he loves.

Betty J. Eadie, author of the book *Embraced by the Light,* also reports about a journey to other spheres when she had a near-death experience connected to an operation in 1973.

Betty was the seventh child of ten in a family where the father was "a blond man of Scottish-Irish descent" and the mother was a Sioux-Indian woman.

Her parents separated when Betty was four years old. Six of the children were placed at a Catholic boarding school where forty girls slept together in a large dormitory. When she was five years old, she got whooping cough and double pneumonia at the same time, so the doctors doubted she would survive the illness.

One day she heard the doctor say: "It's too late. We have lost her," Then Betty felt that they pulled up the sheet over her head.

Although the sheet was over her face, Betty was able to see the doctor and the nurse standing by the bed. She saw that the room was filled with a very bright light and soon she felt that she no longer was lying in bed, but in someone's arms. She saw that it was a man with a beautiful white beard who was holding her. She was fascinated by the man's beard that seemed to sparkle a bright light that came from within his beard. He cradled her in his arms and, although Betty did not know who he was, she felt happy being in his arms. Then she heard the nurse shout: "She breathes again!"

After recovering, Betty wondered who the man with the white beard had been, but no one could give her any answer as none of the nurses or doctors hold her in the arms as she was thought to be dead.

"The memory of my experience has never faded, and every time I think about it, I get the same feeling of security and happiness I felt in his arms," Betty said later.

Betty writes about the years at the boarding school and the image of God she received during her childhood.

"On Sunday all of the children attended church, which offered my sisters and me the possibility of seeing our brothers on the other side of the chapel.

As I fought through the crush of girls to get a glimpse of my brothers that first Sunday, I felt a knock on my head. I turned around and saw a long pole with a rubber ball on the end. The Sisters used this instrument to correct our behavior in church, and this would be only the first of many times I felt it. Because I found it difficult to understand what the bells meant and when I should kneel, I was tapped by the pole often. Still, though, I was able to see my brother, and this was worth any punishment from the ball.

We were taught about God there, and I learned many things I had never considered. We were told that we-the Indians-were heathens and sinners, and, of course, I believed this. The nuns were supposed to be special in God's eyes, and we learned that they were there to help us. My sister Thelma was often beaten by them with a little hose and was then forced to thank the Sister who had done it or be beaten again." ((Embraced by the Light, page 8–9)

Betty learned "to fear God":

"… I began to fear God immensely … Everything I learned about him intensified this fear. He seemed angry and impatient and very powerful, which meant that he would probably destroy me or send me straight to hell on Judgment Day – or before then if I crossed him. This boarding-school god was a being I hoped never to meet. (page 9)

During summers I attended both Lutheran and Baptist churches and occasionally the Salvation Army.

Where I attended church then did not seem as important as the fact that I went. My curiosity about God grew as I matured because I recognized that he was playing a major role in my life. I just was not sure what that role was or how it would affect me as I grew older. I approached him in prayer to get answers, but I did not feel that he heard me. My words just seemed to dissipate in the air. When I was eleven I summoned my courage and asked our school matron if she really believed that there was a god. I felt that if anybody really knew, she did. But instead of answering my question, she slapped me and asked how dare I question his existence. She told me to get to my knees and pray for forgiveness, which I did. But now I knew that I was doomed to hell because of my lack of faith – because I had questioned the existence of God. I was sure now that I could never be forgiven." (page 11)

The negative experiences of religion and Church has deeply influenced Betty's faith. She continued to pray and search for the true nature of God, but instead of trust, she felt fear for God.

"My search for the true nature of God continued. I remember attending various churches and memorizing many scriptures from the New Testament. I came to believe that when a person died, his spirit would remain in the grave with the body until resurrection day, when Christ

would come and the righteous would rise up to be with him. I thought of this often, still dreading my own death and the blackness that would follow." (Embraced by Light, page 12)

On 18 November 1973, when Betty got a near-death experience, she realized that she had got wrong and false information about God and Jesus at the boarding school and in different churches where she used to attend the Sunday service. She realized that she did not need fear God and she should not wait until the Day of Judgment to see Jesus, as Christian priests teach and assert it.

"*It was the evening of 18 November 1973. I had been put in the hospital to undergo a hysterectomy. As a thirty-year mother of seven children and otherwise in excellent health, I had chosen to obey my doctor's advice and go with the surgery,*" says Betty (page 17)

In the evening the day she had been operated, she dozed for a while, but then she suddenly woke up with a strange feeling.

I felt a terrible sinking sensation, like the very last drops of blood were being drained from me. I heard a soft buzzing sound in my head and continued to sink until I felt my body become still and lifeless.

Then I felt a surge of energy. It was almost as if I felt a pop or release inside me, and my spirit was suddenly drawn out through my chest and pulled upwards, as if by a giant magnet. My first impression was that I was free. There was nothing unnatural about my experience. I was above the bed, hovering near the ceiling.

*I turned and saw a body lying on the bed. I was curious about who it was, and immediately I began descending toward it … An then I recognized that it was my own. That was **my body** on the bed. I wasn't taken aback, and I wasn't frightened; I simply felt a kind of sympathy for it. It appeared younger and prettier than I remembered, and now it was dead. **It was as if I had taken off a used garment and had put it aside forever …** (page 29)*

*My new body was weightless and extremely mobile, and I was fascinated by my new state of being. **Although I had felt pain from the*** *surgery only moments before, I now felt no discomfort at all. I was whole in every way – perfect. And I thought, 'This is who I really am*

'I'm dead,' I thought, 'and no one is here to know it!' But before I could move, three men suddenly appeared at my side. They wore beautiful, light brown robes … A kind of glow emanated from them, but not unusually bright, and then I realized that a soft glow came from my own body and that our lights had merged together around us. I was not afraid …

They had been with me for 'eternities,' they said. I didn't fully understand this; I had a difficult time comprehending the concept of eternity, let alone eternities. Eternity to me had always been in the future, but these beings said they had been with me for eternities in the past. This was more difficult to comprehend. Then I began to see images in my mind of a time long ago, of an existence before my life on earth, of my relationship with these men 'before' … The fact of a pre-earth life crystallized in my mind, and I saw that death was actually a 'rebirth' into a greater life of understanding and knowledge that stretched forward and backward through time … They explained that they, with others, had been my guardian angels during my life on earth …

They said that I had died prematurely. They somehow communicated a feeling of peace and told me not to worry, that everything would be all right … I sensed their deep love and concern. These feelings and other thoughts were communicated from spirit to spirit – from intelligence to intelligence … (page 30 … 33)

Betty traveled through a black mass that soon took on the shape of a tunnel. Then she saw a pinpoint of light in the distance and **noticed the figure of a man standing in it, with the light radiating all around him** (page 40)

"*I felt my light being drawn to his. It was as if there were two lamps in a room, both shining, their light merging together …*

And as our lights merged, I felt as if I had stepped into his countenance, and I felt an utter explosion of love.

It was the most unconditional love I have ever felt, and as I saw his arms open to receive me I went to him and received his complete embrace and said over and over, **'I'm home.** *I'm home. I'm finally home.'* **I felt**

his enormous spirit and knew that I had always been a part of him. ... *I knew that he was aware of all my sins and faults, but that they didn't matter right now ...*

There was no questioning who he was. I knew that he was my Savior, and friend, and God. He was Jesus Christ, who had always loved me, even when I thought he hated me.

All my life I had feared him, and I now saw – I knew – that he was my choicest friend. Gently, he opened his arms ... and said: 'Your death was premature, it is not yet your time.' ... Now, within his words, I felt a mission, a purpose; I didn't know what it was, but I knew that my life on earth had not been meaningless.

It was not yet my time.

My time would come when my mission, my purpose, my meaning in this life was accomplished. I had a reason for existing on earth. But even though I understood this, my spirit rebelled. Did this mean I would have to go back? I said to him, 'No, I can never leave you now.' (page 40 ... 43)

Betty describes the process of "dying" in a simple but fascinating way reminding us Jesus' experience on the cross. *"When we 'die', my guides said, we experience nothing more than a transition to another state. Our spirits slip from the body and move to a spiritual realm. If our deaths are traumatic, the spirit quickly leaves the body, sometimes even before death occurs. If a person is in an accident or fire, for example, their spirit may be taken from their body before they experience much pain. The body may actually appear still alive for some moments, but the spirit will have already left ..."* (page 83)

Betty asserts *"that it is important for us to acquire knowledge of the spirit while we are in the flesh. The more knowledge we acquire here, the further and faster we will progress there. Because of lack of knowledge or belief, some spirits are virtual prisoners of this earth. Some who die as atheists, or those who have bonded to the world through greed, bodily appetites, or other earthly commitments find it difficult to move on, and they become earth-bound."* (page 84)

NEAR-DEATH EXPERIENCES

Research on near-death experience began in the 1970's by pure chance.

In 1943, at the age of 20, **George Ritchie, Jr., M.D.** (1923–2007) was a private in the Army stationed in Texas. He was awaiting a transfer to Richmond to study medicine at the Medical College of Virginia to become a doctor for the military. However, he got sick with pneumonia and died. The army physician in charge, who could not detect any evidence of respiration or cardiac impulse, declared Ritchie dead.

According to later accounts of Dr. Ritchie, only his physical body was "dead"; in reality he was more alive than ever. He experienced that he left his body and could wander around the hospital. As he was not aware of his physical dead, he found it strange that no one could see him. He returned to his room and recognized his lifeless body, which had been covered with a sheet. Suddenly the room became bright and George Ritchie found himself in the presence of Jesus who guided him through several realms of the afterlife.

He could see **spirits in the realm closest to Earth**. Many of them were acting like still being on the Earth, as they did not understand that they were dead.

Another realm he was shown **was a kind of "receiving station", where spirits would arrive in a deep hypnotic sleep**. There were spirits of people who believed that they had to "sleep" in their grave until the second coming of Christ and until angel Gabriel came along blowing on a horn. Jesus told George Ritchie that this happened because these people had believed in the teaching of the Christian church about waiting for the Judgment Day when Christ "will come to judge the living and the dead", and that it was wrong. Heavenly beings tried to arouse these people and help them to realize that God is truly a God of the living and that they did not have to wait.

In another realm George Ritchie could see hordes of spirits who are the most miserable and angriest beings. These **spirits were locked into destructive thought-patterns, rage and uncontrollable lust.** Jesus did not condemn them, but had very great compassion for them. It was not easy to help them as these "dark" spirits fled from the light as they were afraid of being revealed.

He caught then a glimpse of another **realm where he saw a building similar to an enormous university** where spirits dressed as monks busily were engaged in some form of research. These were the spirits of people who grew beyond selfish desires while on Earth, but these spirits were not able to see Jesus either.

George Ritchie was taken into outer space there **he experienced a brilliant light.** He got the information that people, who have become like Jesus while on Earth, have the chance to go to this place. He realized that this was heaven, but he was not allowed to enter it; he was told to return to his physical body. At this point, he was revived from death. The ward, who was preparing Ritchie's body for the morgue, detected movement in his chest and called for a medical officer who provided a shot of adrenaline to the patient's heart causing him to breathe and his heart to beat.

George Ritchie returned to life with one of the most important and profound near-death experiences. Later he published his first book, *Return from Tomorrow,* co-authored by Elizabeth Sherill.

Raymond Moody, who had listened to Dr. Ritchie reporting about his near-death experience, got interested in this phenomenon and began documenting similar accounts of people who experienced clinical death. After having released his best-selling book, *Life After Life* (1975), he has become widely known for his research about near-death experiences (NDE).

He had spent decades with inquiring people who had had near-death experience, so finally he was able to outline nine elements that generally occur during NDE. He concluded that people coming from different countries and cultures, belonging to different religions, give similar reports concerning the different moments of the near-death experience. However, there are not many persons reporting a full near-death experience with all the elements/moments.

The first thing a dying person experiences is hearing a strange sound, a buzzing, or ringing noise. One may be in intense pain, but as soon as one leaves the body the pain vanishes.

Many people tell about the sensation of rising up and floating above the physical body and experiencing the spiritual body as a sort of living energy field.

The next experience is that of being drawn into darkness through a tunnel, at an extremely high speed, until they reach a realm of radiant golden-white light. However, some people report rising directly into heaven without having any tunnel experience.

Those people who could see the realm of light say that they met celestial beings reflecting inner light.

Meeting friends and relatives who have passed away is another experience they talk about.

Some people report about meeting a powerful celestial being who helped them to make a review of their lives on earth. Depending on which cultural and religious background the dying person has, this celestial being is identified as God, Jesus,

Allah or some other religious figure. Atheists often call the celestial being *The Being of Light*.

The Being of Light presents the dying with **a panoramic review of everything they have ever done** during their life on Earth. This review occurs not only by reliving the acts, but even feeling the positive or negative influence of the acts on the people these were directed to.

The dying person is often told that he/she must return to the life on Earth, but in some cases the dying person is given a choice of either staying in the other dimension or returning to Earth. Most of the people are reluctant to return.

"*I knew I was dying and that there was nothing I could do about it, because no one could hear me*" a person said when being interviewed by Doc. Moody. "*I was out of my body, there's no doubt about it, because I could see my own body there on the operation room table. My soul was out! All this made me feel very bad at first, but then, this really bright light came. It did seem that it was a little dim at first, but then it was this huge beam. It was just a tremendous amount of light, nothing like a big bright flashlight. It was just too much light. And it gave off heat to me; I felt a warm sensation.*

It was a bright yellowish white – more white. It was tremendously bright; I just can't describe it. It seemed that it covered everything, yet it didn't prevent me from seeing everything around me – the operating room, the doctors and nurses, everything. I could see clearly, and it wasn't blinding.

At first, when the light came, I wasn't sure what was happening, but then, it asked, it kind of asked me if I was ready to die. I was like talking to a person, but a person wasn't there. The light's what was talking to me, but in a voice.

Now, I think that the voice that was talking to me actually realized that I wasn't ready to die. You know, it was just kind of testing me more than anything else. Yet, from the moment the light spoke to me, I felt really good – secure and loved. The love which came from it is just unimaginable, indescribable. It was a fun person to be with! And it had a sense of humor, too – definitely!"

Skeptics who tend to reject all supernatural phenomena, often doubt near-deaths experiences recounted in books, but all skepticism is dispersed when one listens personally to somebody who self has got that experience. This happened to me when I heard László (assumed name) telling about his accident and out-of-body experience.

In 1989, at the end of October my mum called and told me that my beloved father had passed away. She urged me to take the plane from Copenhagen to Budapest as soon as possible, as the burial should take place after maximum four days according to our tradition in Transylvania (Rumanian). László, a relative to my sister-in-law collected me from the airport in Budapest and drove me to the nearest border crossing to my hometown Szatmár (Satu Mare located in northwestern Transylvania).

Although I was sad and heartbroken because of my dad's death, I tried to be polite and conversed with László. Our journey took several hours so we could talk about many items, including the hot political situation in Eastern Europe that led to the fall of communism that autumn. While chatting, Laszló surprised me with a question.

"What do you think of life after death?" he asked while scrutinizing my reaction on the question. As I was traveling to my father's burial, it was not the right moment for me to discuss the topic, so I tried to reply his question briefly: "I do not only believe in life after death, but I even know that we continue to live in another dimension."

László was quiet for a while and then he said: "Basically I've got the same opinion."

He told me that he was Catholic but used to attend Mass seldom as he had to work a lot with his farming and fruit growing. However, he has had many thoughts about God and about an event in his youth that he never dared to tell anyone about. He now wanted to hear what I thought of his experience that occurred when he was 23 years old.

At that time László used to drive a motorcycle, as he could not afford a car. One day when he was driving on a small, bumpy village-road with many bushes and trees alongside, he happened to run into a large flock of sheep in a curve. He had no time to brake and therefore the accident was unavoidable.

László did not feel any pain when the accident occurred. Although he was unconscious, he had strong memories of the ambulance that took him to the hospital and of the villagers who stood horrified by the accident. All this he saw from above while he "floated" above the ambulance and the people.

At the hospital László experienced that he could move "through closed doors and the walls," as he put it. One moment he experienced being in the room where doctors were fighting for his life, the next moment he "float" to the waiting room where his parents were desperate of fear to lose him. When he wanted to comfort them, he realized that he could not get contact with them as they did not hear or see him.

When László got back his consciousness, he would have liked to talk about his out-of-body experience, but, as his family was Catholic, he knew that nobody would have believed his account. He decided not to tell to anybody about his experience. However, now, more than 20 years after the accident, he was surprised and happy to hear that many people have got similar experience and that research of the phenomena is going on.

Near-death experiences have occurred both in past times and present, but the fear of being labeled as a person with crazy fantasies or of being told that the experience was the evil work of Satan, has prevented people of different cultures and religions to talk about what they had experienced in connection with a serious illness or devastating accident.

Eva Malmberg, a member of the church I was in service for several years, was in her eighties when she dared to talk about her near-death experience she had had when being a young teacher in a small town in Sweden.

Eva was about 22 or 23 years old when she fell off the bike and hit her head badly, while riding her bicycle too fast downhill on a village-road. As she immediately lost consciousness, she felt no pain. Suddenly she found herself sitting on a rock, at some distance from the place of the accident, and watching the ambulance that collected her body. When the ambulance drove to the hospital, she was floating above it.

Despite her being in unconscious state, Eva observed the doctors "working" with her lacerated body. She soon discovered that she was able to move through walls and she saw her parents sitting in the waiting room and weeping.

After several days of unconsciousness, Eva came back to a conscious life.

A few years after the accident Eva moved to Lund, a university city in South Sweden. Here she decided to contact a priest and talk about her remarkable near-death experience that she still was often thinking about. But the priest doubted her story and told her to: "Keep quiet about this. It is Satan who has given you these thoughts. "

Although Eva felt insulted and rejected, she obeyed the recommendation of the priest not to talk about her experience. However, as she lost her confidence in priests and the church, she did not attend any service during more than 50 years.

Listening to or reading about people's near-death experience is fascinating but experiencing self the phenomenon is more convincing. At the beginning of July in 1997, I had an emergency operation on a tumor that had severely affected my physical ability.

Eight days after the operation I wanted to leave the hospital even though doctors warned me for being too weak to take care of myself at home.

I took no medicines as I wanted to let my body to recover in a natural way.

Twelve days after the operation, early in the morning while I still was in bed, I suddenly felt that I was "falling" like in a kind of emptiness. Next moment I was aware that I was out-of-my body and was floating around in the apartment. There was a very bright light all around me and I felt that a strong energy, like a magnet was pulling me through the living room and the hall while I was fighting against it. "I do not want to die, I still have so much to do," I explained in a non-verbal way to the invisible force that was pulling me.

Then I felt that the "force" released me, and suddenly I was back in the room where my body was lying in bed. I physically felt that I slipped back into my body, such as a hand is sliding into a glove.

I was overwhelmed when I realized that I could have died. At the same time I was thankful for my experiencing the two nature of my life: the physical and the spiritual one.

After my experience, I started to read about near death experience, and was surprised to learn that the phenomenon was more common as I had thought before. It has also helped me to give a new interpretation to some stories about Jesus arising people who were thought to be dead. We read in The Gospel of Luke about Jairus, a ruler of the synagogue who asked Jesus to come to his house and help his dying daughter. While they were talking, Jairus got the bad news that his daughter had already died. Hearing this, Jesus comforts Jairus by saying him: "Do not be afraid; only believe, and she will be made well."

"So it was, when Jesus returned, that the multitude welcomed him, for they were all waiting for him.

And behold, there came a man named Jairus, and he was a ruler of the synagogue. And he fell down at Jesus' feet and begged him to come to his house, for he had an only daughter about twelve years of age, and she was dying ...

While he was still speaking, someone came from the ruler of the synagogue's house, saying to him, 'Your daughter is dead. Do not trouble the Teacher.'

But when Jesus heard it, he answered him, saying, 'Do not be afraid; only believe, and she will be made well.'

When he came into the house, he permitted no one to go in except Peter, James, and John, and the father and mother of the girl.

Now all wept and mourned for her; but he said, 'Do not weep; she is not dead, but sleeping.'

And they laughed him to scorn, knowing that she was dead.

But he put them all out, took her by the hand and called, saying, 'Little girl, arise.'

Then her spirit returned, and she arose immediately. And he commanded that she be given something to eat.

And her parents were astonished, but he charged them to tell no one what had happened." Luke 8:40 ... 56)

Skeptical scientists say that near-death experiences may be caused by lack of oxygen to the brain or by drugs, or stress evoked by fear of death. Doctor *Melvin Morse* contests this opinion when he writes in the preface to Betty J. Eadies book the following thoughts on the near-death experience:

"Near-death experiences are not caused by a lack of oxygen to the brain, or drugs, or psychological stresses evoked by the fear of dying. Almost twenty years of scientific research has documented that these experiences are a natural and normal process. We have even documented an area in the brain which allows us to have the experience. That means that near-death experiences are absolutely real and not hallucinations of the mind. They are as real as any other human capability; they are as real as math, as real as language ... Unfortunately, our society has not yet accepted the scientific advances in understanding the dying process which have occurred in the past two decades. We desperately need to reeducate ourselves that we are spiritual beings as well as biological machines." (Foreword for Betty J. Eddie's book, Embraced By The Light)

People who have had near-death experience, do not want to interpret, but only to talk about the experience. Even if their words are almost inadequate to describe the indescribable, these people witness the same thing that Jesus teaches, that we are spiritual beings living in a physical body and that our "real home" is not Earth but another realm of the universe.

HUMANS

People in the past and present have discussed and tried to answer existential questions like: – What is the origin of life, and who are we, humans on the whole?
 – Why is the human body so fragile and vulnerable?
 – Why does God allow suffering?

These are general existential questions that arise especially when one is confronting incurable illness, one is growing older or when a beloved person dies.

All religions have got one or perhaps several stories about the origin of human life. Although the depiction of the creation process is different, the common recurrent pattern in the different creation stories is that humans are created of clay and that a "spirit" inhabits the "clay" figure.
  In the Sumerian *Gilgamesh Epic,* written at least one thousand year before *Genesis* (Bible), we read about **a goddess**, called **Mami** (Mama) who was involved in the creation of humans. As Nintu legends states she pinched off fourteen pieces of **primordial clay** which she formed into womb deities who **produced seven pairs of human embryos.** According to the epic, the gods decided to slay one among them and to use that god's blood and flesh, mixed with clay, to create humans.

There are two creation stories in *the Bible* indicating that the editors have used different sources and traditions.

According to the first story, God was not alone when creating the man, but he interacted with one or more gods who were admonished to cooperate:

"Then God said, 'Let us make man in **our** image, according to our likeness ... So God created man in his **own** image; in the image of God he created him; male and female he created them." (Genesis 1:26 ... 27)

The other creation story in *Genesis* expresses a dualistic view of life as the author does not report only about the creation of the matter-body but also about "the breath of life", the spirit that was breathed into the nostrils of the "dust-figure".

*"And **the LORD GOD formed man of the dust of the ground, and breathed into his nostrils the breath of life; and man became a living being ...**"(Genesis 2:7)*

According to the second story, the woman was not created simultaneously with the man, but she was later fashioned out of the ribs of Adam in order to be his helper.

"And the LORD God said: 'It is not good that man should be alone; I will make him a helper comparable to him.' ... And the LORD GOD caused a deep sleep to fall on Adam, and he slept; and he took one of his ribs, and closed up the flesh in its place. Then the rib which the LORD GOD had taken from man he made into a woman, and he brought her to the man." (Genesis 2:18 ... 22)

Scientists claim that the biblical texts as well as the Sumerian Gilgamesh Epic present a very simplified picture of the creation process. They reject them as "non-scientific" without taking into consideration that even these stories contain "scientific" observations, as the physical body partially is a "clay body" containing many elements of the earth. A newborn child's body, for instance, is made up of about 70% water and of many other components of "the dust of the ground", as minerals, iron, zinc, phosphorus, and so on. When scientists talk about the chemicals of the body, in fact they refer to elements existing in the "dust of the ground". Even if biologists and chemists never mention about "the breath of life", it is known that a human being is not able to be alive without the "spirit of life".

When discussing the origin of humans in ancient times, it was a central philosophical issue and a matter of course to have a dualistic view of life according to which humans have both a matter and a spirit "body".

Plato (427–347 BC.), one of the world's best known Greek philosophers, was a dualist who thought that everything created in our world has got a preexisting *"parallel model"* as a kind of *"idea"* or *"immaterial form"* in another sphere of the universe. He thought that the pre-existent forms/ideas are universal, eternal, immaterial and more real than the material things we know by senses. He thought that the human's soul (in Plato's interpretation even called "mind") exists already before birth and that after birth it is supplied with knowledge from the invisible "world of the ideas". He did not believe that the soul was dependent on the physical body.

Plato talks of the divine as *reason* – *logos* in Greek. Logos is the divine principle that organizes the eternal, immaterial universe that can take form in the visible matter world.

Knowledge about the true nature of the universe was important also for **Plotinos** (205–270 AD), a "mystical" thinker who studied philosophy in Alexandria and then moved to Rome. He thought that the universe is stretched out between two poles: the divine light, that he called The One, and darkness, that he considered to be the absence of light.

Plotinos developed a complex spiritual cosmology involving three elements: The One, the Mind (Intelligence) and the Soul. According to him, it is from the productive unity of these three "Beings" that all existence emanates. Concerning the soul, Plotinos thought that it is composed of a higher and a lower part. The higher part is unchangeable and divine and aloof from the lower part, yet providing the lower part with life. He considered humans as souls employing a body as an instrument for a temporary life on Earth. The highest part of a person is one's own intellect/soul that is eternal.

According to Plotinos The One, the "Good" or the "Divine Mind" is beyond the power of words to describe; it was never created, and can never be destroyed.

He believed that evil is caused by our attachment to the things of this world that prevent our complete devotion to the Divine Mind. The objects of our desires and affections are not in themselves bad as long as they do not prevent us to attain **the purpose of our lives: realizing the existence of Divine Mind/The One.**

Plotinos says that one's goal in life should be a mystical union with the Divine Mind and he claimed that he had attained this union himself four times in his life.

Another philosopher who considered **the mind** being **non-physical** and therefore of non-spatial-substance, was **René Descartes** (1641). He identified the mind with consciousness and self-awareness and distinguished this from the brain as the seat of intelligence.

"Cogito, ergo sum" (Latin), that means "I think, thus I am" is his well-known phrase that summarizes the essence of his philosophy.

A contemporary to Descartes was the German rationalist **Gottfried Wilhelm Leibniz** (1646–1716).

Leibniz talks about God and about non-composite, immaterial, soul-like entities called "monads". Space, time, causation, material objects – are all illusions according to his philosophy. He thinks that material things such as machines or brains cannot possibly have mental states. Only immaterial things, soul-like entities, are able to think or perceive; our minds must be immaterial and we must have souls in order to be aware of the universe.

Leibniz denies any genuine interaction between soul and body. My foot moves when I decide to move it, as well as I can feel pain when my body is injured, but this cannot be explained by a casual influence of my soul on my body, or of my body on my soul.

He also rejects the idea that God continually intervenes in order to produce the correspondence between my soul and body. That would be unworthy of God, according to Leibniz. God has created my soul and my body in such a way that they naturally correspond to each other, without any divine intervention. My foot moves when I decide to move it because this motion has been programmed into it from the beginning. I feel pain when my body is injured because this pain was programmed into my soul.

Immanuel Kant, leaves the question of dualism open. Whether the soul is immortal or not, whether we are free or determined, whether the world is infinite or not, all of these are so called "antinomies reasons". He means that we can use reason to support either view. The question if humans are dualistic or merely material is irresolvable according to I. Kant, who was basically interested in reconciling religion with science.

While philosophers and scientists tried to find plausible explanations of the origin of life, the institutional Christian church was fighting against them, showing intolerance against those who had new views and theories about creation and Heaven and Earth.

As a reaction to the intolerance of the Church and the acts of the Inquisition, new philosophical trends as naturalism and materialism appeared. Unfortunately, some scientists had to pay with their life for their new theories that were rejected as heresies by the Catholic Court of Inquisition.

According to **naturalism**, only natural (as opposed to supernatural or spiritual) laws and forces operate in the world. The naturalists assert that natural laws govern the whole structure of the universe.

During **Enlightenment** a number of philosophers including Voltaire and Francis Bacon, rejected believing in supernatural forces and outlined only philosophical justifications when investigating the natural world.

Materialism is a form of philosophical monism which holds that matter is the fundamental substance in nature, and that all things, including mental things and consciousness, are results of material interactions. To materialists, matter is primary, and mind or spirit or ideas are secondary, being a product of matter acting upon matter.

Actually, materialism is not a new philosophical trend; it existed already in ancient time in several geographically separated regions of Eurasia. In Ancient Indian philosophy for example, materialism was developed around 600 years before Christ.

In Ancient China, Confucian doctrines (ca 312 BC) centered on realism and materialism.

Greek ancient philosophers like Thales, Epicurus and Democritus prefigure later materialists.

Charles Darwin (born 1809) tried to find out the origin of life in general and of the human life in particular. During five years on board the ship Beagle, which was mapping the coast of South America, Darwin took thousands of samples and specimens and later, while working on these, he started to think about the origin of species. After more than twenty years of research he finally published his new theory of "**evolution by natural selection**".

Later he worked on a book about the evolution of humanity and the role of sexual selection. In **Descent of Man,** published in 1871, he claimed that humans were descended from animals. His theory consists of two main points: 1. diverse groups of animals evolve from one or a few common ancestors; 2. the mechanism by which this evolution takes place is natural selection. He asserted that only strong species of plants, animals and humans are able to adapt to the environment and survive while the other ones have no chance.

Even if Darwin did his best to find out the truth about the origin of life generally and of the human specifically, there were several questions that he was not able to answer. Haeckel, a contemporary scientist to Darwin, considered his research uncompleted and wrote the following criticism:

"The chief defect of the Darwinian theory is that it throws no light on the origin of the primitive organism – probably a simple cell – from which all the others have descended. When Darwin assumes a special creative act for this first species, he is not consistent (Haeckel, 1862)

Darwin's opinion about the origin of life varied somewhat during his life, and finally he realized that the mystery of life and of matter surpassed the scientists' capacity to give credible explanations. He believed in God, the Creator who, according to Darwin's opinion, is involved in the process of evolution.

Belief in spontaneous generation of certain forms of life from non-living matter goes back to Aristotle and ancient Greek philosophy and continued to have support in Western scholarship until the nineteenth century. However, there were several scientists who refuted the evolution theory. In 1861, **Louis Pasteur** for example, performed a series of experiments that demonstrated that organisms such as bacteria and fungi do not spontaneously appear by themselves in sterile, nutrient-rich media. He concluded that life originates from somewhere else in the universe. His theory was rejected by several scientists who thought that this approach asserted "the operation of metaphysical, spiritual entities" and that it turns on the argument of creation by design by a creator or demiurge". (Bernal)

According to **Fred Hoyle** (1915–2001), a famous astronomer and mathematician, the probability of arising by chance a living cell from lifeless matter on Earth, is not as big as the probability that a hurricane would assemble a working Boeing 747 while sweeping through a scrap yard.

Giuseppe Sermonti, Italian biologist says that it is hardly believable that chance and natural selection could form a dinosaur from an amoeba.

Most research in modern times has been focused on the "matter-body". Biologists and physicists talk about living cells originating from lifeless matter without having managed yet to prove, despite advanced technical equipment, that their theory is correct.

Scientists researching the "clay-body" concentrate on the visible physical figure of humans and do not have much to say about man's thoughts and feelings, about soul, spirit and consciousness that is the invisible, yet very real part of man. Their instruments are not suited to explore all the aspects and mysteries of the human existence. Nor can their largest space telescopes give us right information and knowledge of the universe or of multiple universes. Why? Perhaps because their earthly, matter- instruments are suited only to the physical world that we are able to perceive. As they cannot reach beyond the frequency bands of the visible and palpable world, the most important existential questions concerning creation are not yet scientifically answered.

Are we, humans only a clod of cells, of chemical substances and subatomic particles? Are we really only "clay" figures or are we more complex beings?

WHAT JESUS TEACHES ABOUT THE CREATION

Unfortunately, there are no texts in the New Testament revealing Jesus' doctrines concerning the creation of humans. As Luke and Mark, the authors of synoptic gospels in the New Testament, were not disciples of Jesus, they missed the Master's teaching about existential issues.

It is the text collection found in Nag Hammadi that presents "the philosopher" Jesus who surprises the disciples and the Jews with a creation story totally different from the one we read in the Old Testament. He talks about an original human "model" existing in another sphere/dimension and he also reports about spheres where copies of the original "model" were created. The scribes and Pharisees were upset when listening to his new doctrines that contradicted their belief.

When Mary puts questions concerning the distinction of the perishable and imperishable things, the Master presents a rather complicated and dramatic story of creation. He talks about the Lord of the universe, called Forefather whose image is the Father of mankind.

"*The Lord of the universe is addressed not as Father but as Forefather. <The Father is> the beginning of those who will appear, but the Lord is the Forefather without a beginning.*"(NH, The Wisdom of Christ: 98,9 ... page 98,9)

The Father is "*as old as the light before him but not as powerful. Afterward there was revealed a multitude of beings, just as old and powerful, who are self-conceived and reflective. Glorious and without number ... You yourselves have appeared from the people of this generation,"(NH, The Wisdom of Jesus Christ: 98,9)* says Jesus to the disciples who certainly listened astonished.

When Matthew asks how Humanity was revealed, Jesus says that an immortal androgynous Human was the first "model" in the realm of the light.

"Matthew said to him, 'Master, how was Humanity revealed?'

The perfect Savior said, 'I want you to know that the being who appeared before the universe in infinity is the one who grows by himself, the self-made Father. He is full of bright light and ineffable. In the beginning, when he decided to turn his likeness into a great power, at once the strength of that light appeared as an immortal androgynous Human ... "

"The first Human has a mind of his own within, and thought, appropriate to him, and consideration, reflection, reason and power.

All these attributes are perfect and immortal. They are equally imperishable but not equally powerful. They are different, like the difference between father and son, <and son> and thought, and thought and the rest.

As I said before about what was produced, the One is first. ... all that was revealed came from his power. From what was created came what was fashioned. From what was fashioned came what was formed. From what was formed came what was named. This is how differences came to be among what was unconceived, from beginning to end." (NH, The Wisdom of Jesus Christ 100,16 ... page 291)

The history of mankind starts when a female entity called Wisdom (Sophia in Greek) wants to create something by herself without the consent of the Spirit; her action caused a *Defect* in the perfect and harmonious realm of the One, the Light.

"Now, Sophia, who is the Wisdom of Insight and who constitutes an aeon, ... wanted to bring forth something like herself, without the consent of the Spirit, who had not given approval, without her partner and without his consideration".(NH, The Secret Book of John 9,25 ...

page 114) "Something came out of her that was imperfect and different in appearance from her, for she had produced it without her partner. It did not resemble its mother and was misshapen." (NH, The Secret Book of John, The Fall of Sophia, page 114..)

When Sophia realizes her mistake, she gets scared and sad. She hides her creation in a bright cloud *"so that no one would see it except the holy Spirit, who is called the Mother of the living. She named her offspring Yaldabaoth." (NH, The Secret Book of John,*
The Fall of Sophia, 9,25 ... page 114 ... 115)

Sophia's light diminished and she was ashamed. *"She repented with many tears. The whole realm of Fullness heard her prayer of repentance and offered prays on her behalf to the Invisible Virgin Spirit and the Spirit consented ... the holy Spirit poured upon her some of the fullness of all ... She was taken up not to her own eternal realm, but instead to a position above her son. She was to remain in the ninth heaven until she restored what was lacking in herself." (The Secret Book of John; Sophia Repents13,13 ... , page 117 ... 118)*

Sophia's "offspring", Yaldabaoth starts creating his own spheres (aeons) using the power he has got from his mother. According to gnostic scriptures Jesus called this half-god, half-demon entity "the first ruler", "the ruler of the world", "the rubber", "the child of the chaos", the "blind god" as well as "the arrogant". Yaldabaoth is also called Sakla and Samael in the scripts.

"This is first ruler, the archon who took great power from his mother. Then he left her and moved away from the place where he was born. He took control and created for himself other aeons with luminous fire, which still exists. He mated with the mindlessness in him and produced authorities for himself" (The Secret Book of John; 10,10 ... page 115)

Yaldabaoth tried to create and organize everything after the pattern of the highest realm of the One, but his attempt failed in many ways.

"Yaldabaoth organized everything after the pattern of the first aeons that had come into being, so that he might create everything in an incorruptible form. Not that he had seen the incorruptible ones. Rather, the power that is in him, that he had taken from his mother, produced in him the pattern for the world order." (NH, The Secret Book of John, page 117)

After having created his realms, Yaldabaoth declared boastfully: *"I am a jealous god and there is no other god beside me."* (page 117) It is noteworthy that there is a similar text in *Isaiah 45:5 ... 7* according to which the God of Israel declares the same thing about himself:

"I am the LORD, and there is no other;
There is no God besides me."
The almighty God of Israel creates light and darkness and makes peace and causes calamity: *"I form the light and create darkness, I make peace and create calamity; I, the LORD, do all these things."*

Yaldabaoth, who had created his realm of archons and angels, had the ambition to do a copy of the immortal First Human who existed in the highest Realm of the One.

"Yaldabaoth said to the authorities with him, 'Come, let's create a human being after the image of God and with a likeness to ourselves, so that this human image may give us light.'

They created through their respective powers, according to the features that were given. Each of the authorities contributed a psychical feature corresponding do the figure of the image they had seen. They created a being like the perfect first human, and said, 'Let's call it Adam, that its name may give us power of light.'"(The Secret Book of John, The Creation of Adam, 15,1 ... page 119)

Not less than 365 angels worked hardly until, *"limb by limb, the psychical and material body was completed."* However, when they finally finished their work, the archons were disappointed as their creation was like a robot that could not stand up or move. As Yaldabaoth was desperate, the angels said to him: *"Breathe some of your spirit into the face of Adam, and the body will arise.'*

He breathed his spirit into Adam. The spirit is the power of his mother, but he did not realize this, because he lives in ignorance. The Mother's power went out of Yaldabaoth and into the psychical body that had been made to be like the one who is from the beginning."

The body moved and became powerful. And it was enlightened."

According to this creation story, Yaldabaoth and his co-workers became jealous when seeing that their creation, Adam was powerful, enlightened and more intelligent than the creators. Their envy and fear made them to decide to throw "Adam into the lowest part of the whole material realm."

"At once the rest of the powers became jealous. Although Adam came into being through all of them, and they gave their power to this human, Adam was more intelligent than the creators and the first ruler. When they realized that Adam was enlightened and could think more clearly than they and was stripped of evil, they took and threw Adam into the lowest part of the whole material realm." (The Secret Book of John, Adam Receives Spirit and Life: 19,10 ... , page 124 ... 125)

The rulers, Yaldabaoth and his archons, *"brought Adam into the shadow of death"*. They produced *"a figure again, from earth, water, fire, and the spirit that comes from matter – that is, from the ignorance of darkness, and desire, and their own phony spirit. This figure is the cave for remodeling the body that these criminals put on the human, the fetter of forgetfulness. Adam became a mortal person, the first to descend and the first to become estranged."* (The Secret Book of John, page 125)

This creation story is fascinating because Sophia, the entity who wanted to create something by herself as well as Yaldabaoth reminds us of patterns from our world. Man has always had the ambition to create something by copying an existing model. Modern scientists for instance, want to create perfect copies of humans and animals by cloning them, and engineers are building robots which one day could be dangerous for humankind. Yaldabaoth, who creates new worlds in spheres, reminds us of spacemen and astrophysicists searching for planets where humans would be able to live.

Yaldabaoth's and the archon's jealousy and fear also remind us of the jealousy and fear of the rulers of our world. Kings and presidents have imprisoned, tortured and murdered people who were more intelligent and enlightened than they were. The chief priests in Jerusalem, for instance, decided to get rid of Jesus who knew more about the mysteries of God and universe and was more intelligent and enlightened than they were. Popes during the time of Inquisition tortured and murdered scientists or put on them "the fetter of forgetfulness" by keeping them in prison for ever.

Yaldabaoth created even the figure of a female to the image of the first "female model" called Insight or Eve. Jesus said that Yaldabaoth did not create a copy of Eve from "Adam's rib" as Moses said according to the Old Testament, but this creator put a part of "the power of the human being into the female creature."

"The first ruler removed part of Adam's power and created another figure in the form of a female, like the image of Insight that had appeared to him. He put the part he had taken from the power of the human being into the female creature. It did not happen, however, the way Moses said: 'Adam's rib'" (The Secret Book of John, chapter The Creation of Eve (22,28 …)

The idea that we are "copies" of the immortal Human, called Adam or Pigeradamas perplexed and upset the Jewish religious leaders who believed that Adam was created to the likeness of the God of Israel, the Creator.

Many people consider the story of Yaldabaoth, the creator as being pessimistic and unreal. Christian theologians prefer believing in the creation story of the Bible and reject the gnostic scriptures, and scientists consider the theory of evolutionism to be more credible than the creation stories of different religions. However, a closer analysis of all texts and theories reveals that the ancient creation stories and the contemporary scientific theories have got common points. The way of describing the creation process is different but the essence of the theories is similar. Biologists use a scientific language when talking about genetics and heredity and consider each newborn child to be a kind of "copy" of parents and ancestors. They say that humans inherit predisposition to diseases and deficiencies but also good physical and psychical skills from ancestors. When a child is born the parents search after likeness with themselves, the "model", or with someone else in the family. However, this "model" has got its origin in ancestors whose historical roots reach back in infinity. Nobody knows how the first "model" within a family looked like; the newborn, who actually is "a copy of copies", has got DNA and genes of the first "model". Scientists also know that the physical body of man is principally "clay" consisting of water, minerals and other components of the earth.

It is not only Jesus who talks about creation at different levels, but people who were on the other side when having a near-death experience, also report about the multiplicity of the universal creation. Betty J. Eadie, for instance, writes in her book *Embraced by the Light*:

"I saw this process, and then, to further understand it, I was told by the Savior that the spirit creation could be compared to one of our photographic prints; the spirit creation would be like a sharp, brilliant print, and the earth would be like its dark negative. **This earth is only a shadow of the beauty and glory of its creation,** *but it is what we need for our growth …" (page 48)*

"I saw that there are many laws by which we are governed – spiritual laws, and universal laws – most of which we have only an inkling. These laws were created to fulfill a purpose, and all laws complement each other. When we recognize these laws and learn how to use their positive

and negative forces, we will have access to power beyond comprehension. When we break one of these laws, going against that which is the natural order, we have sinned." (page 55)

Taking into account the fascinating complexity of the universe and of the physical human body, one should not underestimate the abilities of the creators, may they be called Yaldabaoth, God of Israel, archons or what-else. These entities surely knew a lot about Earth and the natural conditions on our planet to which the physical body of humans is perfectly adjusted. However, even if these entities had high "technical" knowledge when forming the matter-body, they lacked the right spiritual insight.

The Jewish religious leaders feared that Jesus' new doctrines would turn the people from the traditional religious thinking inherited from the ancestors. We read in *The Secret Book of John* that one day when John went up to the temple, a Pharisee named Arimanios came up to him and said to him:

"'Where is your teacher, whom you followed?'
I said to him, 'He has returned to the place he came from.'
The Pharisee said to me, 'This Nazarene really has deceived you, filled your ears with lies, closed your minds, and turned you from the traditions of your ancestors." (The Secret Book of John: 1,5)

"THE ENLIGHTENED INSIGHT"

There are many similarities between the Creator of The Old Testament and Yaldabaoth as both form the human body of clay, both are boastful when saying "I am a jealous god and there are no other god beside me"; both **prohibit the man and the woman to eat of the tree of the knowledge** as they fear that they will be intelligent and will know what is good and bad. These entities **encourage humans to enjoy the fruits of the tree of life**, which is the material world. According to *The Secret Book of John*, Jesus had not a very good opinion of the "tree of life" planted by Yaldabaoth in the middle of his garden which is Earth. He said: "*The root of their tree is bitter, its branches are death, its shadow is hatred, a trap is in its leaves, its blossom is bad ointment, its fruit is death, desire is its seed, and it blossoms in darkness.*" (NH, The Secret Book of John, page 126.)

When talking about the prohibited fruit of the tree of knowledge, Jesus does not mention Eve as a "sinner" who broke an admonishment. On the contrary, he describes her as his cooperator and Helper who wants to save mankind by supplying knowledge and insight. Eve is the "*enlightened Insight*", the feminine entity who "hides" herself as a spirit in man who has to learn about the true spiritual origin of humanity.

Jesus says that Yaldabaoth, the first ruler wanted to make the minds of the humans "*sluggish, that they may neither understand nor discern,*" (The Secret Book of John, page 126)

We read in The Secret Book of John that Jesus had a dialogue with John about these things. The Master said to him:

"*The first ruler, Yaldabaoth knew Adam was disobedient to him because of enlightened Insight within Adam, which made Adam stronger of mind than he ...*

So he brought deep sleep upon Adam.

I said to the Savior, 'What is deep sleep?'

The Savior said, It is not as Moses wrote and you heard. He said in his first book, 'He put Adam to sleep'. Rather, **this deep sleep was loss of sense.**" (NH, The Secret Book of John, The Imprisonment of Humanity: 20,28 ... page 126)

Jesus says that Eve, also called Insight, appears as light and wants to remove the veil that covers the humans' mind: *"Insight appeared as light and awakened their minds. When Yaldabaoth realized that the humans had withdrawn from him, he cursed his earth ...*

He displayed to his angels the ignorance within him, and he threw the humans out of paradise and cloaked them in thick darkness." (NH, The Secret Book of John, page 127)

According to Jesus, the Mother-Father who "is great in mercy, the holy Spirit, who in every way is compassionate," want to save humans from "the bondage of forgetfulness".

He talks about salvation as a continuous process with a cosmological character involving the celestial Mother-Father who wish to reunite humans with the Whole, as it had been from the beginning before Deficiency occurred. These entities know that Yaldabaoth, the first ruler on Earth has grasped the thoughts of humans.

"Thus all of creation has been blinded so that none might know the God that is over them all. Because of the bondage of forgetfulness, their sins have been hidden. They have been bound with dimensions, times, and seasons, and fate is master of all." (NH, The Secret Book of John, The Human Destiny: 25,15 ...)

The disciples who were listening to the complicated creation story, were sometimes depressed and confused, but Jesus comforted them and gave them hope when saying: *"Power will descend upon every person, for without it no one could stand. After birth, if the spirit of life grows and power comes and strengthens that soul, no one will be able to lead it astray with evil actions. But people upon whom the false spirit descends are misled by it and go astray."* (NH, The Secret Book of John, The Human Destiny: 25,15 … page 129–130)

The scribes and Pharisees definitely rejected the Master's statement that God, the One revealed itself as a "dyad", as Father-Mother. As they lived in a patriarchal society, it was a matter of course to believe in the God of Israel who is always addressed as a man; he is a king, a judge and a creator. It was also unthinkable to accept Eve as a feminine deity because according to their opinion, she was a disobedient "sinner" who, by eating the prohibited fruit of the tree of knowledge, has caused the punishment of mankind. The story of Eve "the sinner" was an existential necessity in their religious concept as it explained the origin of evil and suffering.

It is marveling that Jesus dared to contradict the traditional Jewish opinion about Eve, saying that she is the Mother of All who wants to save mankind by delivering knowledge and insight about the spiritual origin of humans.

Jesus knew that even the disciples had difficulties to abandon the traditional religious thinking and to accept his new doctrines about the "Deficiency" and about the perishable and imperishable. He repeatedly talks about these things in order to help them to understand his purpose. He said:

"I have taught you about the immortal Human, and I have freed him from the fetters of the robbers …

For this reason I have come here, that these may be united with spirit and breath, and two may become one, as in the beginning. *Then you may produce an abundance of fruit and go up to the One who is from the beginning, in ineffable joy and glory and honor and grace of Father of all.*

"Whoever knows the Father in pure knowledge will depart to the Father … Whoever knows him in a defective way will depart to what is defective …"

*"**I have come to eradicate their blindness**, that I might tell everyone about the God who is above all." (The Wisdom of Jesus Christ, The Restoration and Unification of Humanity, BG 8502 121.13 … III 119, 8)*

*"… I took my stand in the midst of the world, and in flesh I appeared to them. I found them all drunk, and I did not find any of them thirsty. **My soul ached for the children of humanity, because they are blind in their hearts and do not see**, for they came into the world empty, and they also seek to depart from the world empty." (The Gospel of Thomas, page 143)*

EVE'S THIRST FOR KNOWLEDGE

If God is good and almighty, why does He permit all the suffering in the world? Is evil a part of God's creation or is it another independent power that wants to shatter the paradisiacal state of Man? The so called *theodicé* problem, i.e. the question of how evil in the world can be consistent with God's existence, has been discussed at length both in philosophy and theology.

The story of Eve's Fall recounted in the Old Testament can be considered as one of many attempts to solve the mystery of suffering and evil. The text was probably written at the turning point of the Jews from polytheism to monotheism, as the author (or authors) tend to assert that both good and evil – even the tempter, the snake – was created by the Lord, the Creator of All.

Eve's "sin" is that even if she knows that it is forbidden to "eat" the fruit of Tree of Knowledge, she breaks the prohibition because of her tempting desire to be wise.

"And the woman said to the serpent, 'We may eat the fruit of the trees of the garden; but of the fruit of the tree which is in the midst of the garden, God has said, ' You shall not eat it, nor shall you touch it, lest you die.'

And the serpent said to the woman, 'You will not surely die. For God knows that in the day you it your eyes will be opened, and you will be like God, knowing good and evil.'

*So when the woman saw that the tree was good for food ... and **a tree desirable to make one wise**, she took its fruit and ate. She also gave to her husband with her, and he ate." (Genesis 3:2–6)*

This story originated in a strictly patriarchal society where women were not supposed to study and get knowledge, so the text was surely used in social context too to legitimize the punishment of women who contradicted the rules. As the question of the origin of evil and sin had to be answered, it was convenient to say that the woman's curiosity caused the "sin", and damaged the good relationship between God and Man.

The punishment of Adam and Eve is very drastic; God does not only drive them out of the Garden of Eden, but He even submits them to pain and sorrow during their life on Earth:

'I will greatly multiply your sorrow and your conception;
In pain you shall bring forth children;
Your desire shall be for your husband,
And he shall rule over you.'
Then to Adam he said, 'Because you have heeded the voice of your wife, and have eaten from the tree of which I commanded you, saying, 'You shall not eat from it':
Cursed is the ground for your sake;
In toil you shall eat from it
All the days of your life'" (Genesis 3:16–17)

Christian theologians have used this story to formulate *the doctrine of the original sin and of evil*. Paul, the Apostle, influenced by and faithful to his former Jewish religious background, uses the story of Eve when formulating his doctrine of justification/salvation. He writes in the Epistle to the Romans:

"Therefore, as through one man's offence, judgment came to all men, resulting in condemnation, even so through one man's righteous act (Jesus' crucifixion) *the free gift came to all men, resulting in justification of life.*

For as by one man's disobedience many were made sinners, so also by one man's obedience many will made righteous." (Romans 5:18–19)

Christian theologians have taken over Paul's strange "judgment and justification" doctrine without considering that **Jesus never talked about Eve's sin and about his crucifixion as a righteous act.**

Even if new translations of the Old Testament make it easier to understand the language of the ancient texts, the story about Eve's sin does not help to solve the difficult existential question why suffering and death exists.

Origines, one of the greatest theologians of the early Christian church, says that every Bible text can be interpreted in different ways: literally, morally, allegorically or spiritually. He also says that the message of the Holy Scripture is hidden from the ordinary reader. No matter which of Origines' interpretation methods we choose, a person without theological background gets confused reading the Genesis text. Presenting the LORD, who is The God of Israel as a revengeful deity who wants to cause pain and suffering does not fit in with the image of The One Supreme Being who loves mankind as Jesus teaches.

There are attempts in the New Testament, especially in the gospel according to Matthew, to put words, expressions and statements into Jesus' mouth that give the impression that he also teaches a strict, punitive and condemning God. However, several researchers of the Old and New Testament as well as of the gospels found in Nag Hammadi point out the different god-images presented in these scripts.

Jesus has a dualistic view of life according to which evil does not belong to the Realm of the Supreme Spirit who is Love, Light and compassion. Evil belongs to the realm of the demons that are powers Jesus fights against. Enlightened Insight, also called Life (she who gives life, i.e. Eve in Hebrew) is the helper whose purpose is to restore humanity to its fullness by uniting all the realms and spheres with the Whole as it was from the beginning.

We read in *The Secret Book of John*:

*"So with its benevolent and most merciful Spirit, the Mother-Father sent a helper to Adam – enlightened Insight, who is from the Mother-Father and who is called Life (*Eve – Hawah in Hebrew means 'she who gives life'*). She helped the whole creature, laboring with it, restoring it to its fullness, teaching it about the descent of the seed, teaching it about the way of ascent, which is the way of descent.*

*Enlightened Insight (*Eve*) was hidden within Adam so that the archons might not recognize her, but that Insight might be able to restore what the Mother (*Sophia*) lacked"* (Nag Hammadi Scriptures, The Secret Book of John: Adam Receives Spirit and Life – 19,10 … 20,28)

Jesus wanted to teach about all these things, and was very upset when Jewish religious leaders tried to stop him. He knew that "hiding the keys of knowledge" was the religious leaders' method of defending their authority and of oppressing people, men and women.

The Master encouraged the disciples to "know themselves" and to learn more about their spiritual origin. He said to them:

"Let one who seeks not stop seeking until one finds. When one finds, one will be troubled. When one is troubled, one will marvel and will reign over all …

When you know yourselves, then you will be known, and you will understand that you are the children of the living Father. But if you do not know yourselves, then you dwell in poverty, and you are poverty." (The Gospel of Thomas, NHC,2, Prologue:2 … 4)

The Master knew that the "ruler of the world", may it be called Yaldabaoth, Sebaoth, Sakla or Satan, had a negative impact on mankind. Scripts teaching about a revengeful and punishing god suggest that, as man is created to the image of such a god, humans have inherited the negative attributes of this creator.

Jesus' purpose was to change the humans' religious thinking and attitude by elevating it to a higher metaphysical level by pointing out the Father in Heaven as the perfect model:

"… YOU SHALL BE PERFECT, JUST AS YOUR FATHER IN HEAVEN IS PERFECT." (Matthew 5:48)

SPIRITUAL KNOWLEDGE

When reading scriptures from old times, may it be the Bible, the Gilgamesh epic, the Koran or other ones, one may wonder how much of the stories are true. As the religious stories and teachings were spread mostly orally in Ancient time, one may suspect that some changes of the original story always occurred. Scriptures of Buddha, who lived in the 500 century BC, were written at least one hundred year after his death. Mohammed, the prophet of Islam lived 570–632 AD, but his biography was not written before 767, that is more than a century after his death. The books of the Old Testament had been written during no less than 1500 years by various authors before being edited at last as one Book.

What about the scriptures reporting about Jesus and his doctrines? There are no preserved first hand manuscripts neither of the texts of the New Testament, nor of the Nag Hammadi scriptures. The researchers first date the copies they have access to and then they approximate the time when the original may have been written. Some of the scriptures, or at least parts of them, were probably recorded by Jesus' closest disciples, or by authors who had listened to the disciples. This "first hand" recording was unusual at that time.

We have learned to get knowledge by reading books written by people who in their turn acquired knowledge and information from other books. Many scientific statements are based on assumptions and abstract mathematical calculations that scientists have learned from books; unfortunately several of such theoretical scientific statements are not always correct as they are not based on real facts.

Neurosurgeon, Doctor Eben Alexander had spent his whole life working hard to accumulate knowledge from books. He adored "the absolute honesty and cleanness of science" as he thought "that it left no room for fantasy or for sloppy thinking." However, later he realizes that *"This approach left very little room for the soul and the spirit, for the continuing existence of a personality after the brain that supported it stopped functioning."* (Eben Alexander, Proof of Heaven – A Neurosurgeon's Journey into the Afterlife)

During his six days being in coma, when his brain did not work at all, he *"was encountering the reality of a world of a consciousness that existed completely free of the limitations of"* his physical brain. He writes: **"My experience showed me that the death of the body and the brain are not the end of consciousness, that human experience continues beyond the grave."** (page 9)

Dr Eben Alexander *"saw the abundance of life throughout the countless universes, including some whose intelligence was advanced far beyond that of humanity." (page 48)*
"*I saw there are countless higher dimensions, but that the only way to know these dimensions is to enter and experience them directly,*" he writes. "*The knowledge given me was not 'taught' in the way that a history lesson or math theorem would be. Insights happened directly … Knowledge was stored without memorization …" (page 49)*
"*Up there, a question would arise in my mind, and the answer would arise at the same time.*
These answers were not simple 'yes' or 'no' fare, either. They were vast conceptual edifices, staggering structures of living thought, as intricate as cities. Ideas so vast they would have taken me lifetimes to find my way around if I had been confined to earthly thought. But I wasn't. I had sloughed off that earthly style of thought like a butterfly breaking from a chrysalis," doctor Alexander recounts in his book. *(page 83)*

After recovering from the devastating disease, doc. Eben Alexander would have liked to share with his family members, friends and medical colleagues all the knowledge he got during his out-of body experience, but he soon realized that it was not a simple task. He still loves physics and cosmology, but now he knows that *"The physical side of the universe is as a speck of dust compared to the invisible and spiritual part."*

"In my past view, spiritual wasn't a word that I would have employed during a scientific conversation. Now I believe it is a word that we cannot afford to leave out," he concludes.

We also read in his book:

"From the Core, my understanding of what we call 'dark energy' and 'dark matter' seemed to have clear explanations, as did far more advanced components of the makeup of our universe that humans won't address for ages …

Perhaps the best way of conveying that part of the experience is to say that I had a foretaste of another, larger kind of knowledge: one I believe human beings will be able to access in ever larger numbers in the future. But conveying that knowledge now is rather like being a chimpanzee, becoming a human for a single day to experience all of the wonders of human knowledge, and then returning to one's chimp friends and trying to tell them what it was like knowing several different Romance languages, the calculus, and the immense scale of the universe." (page 82 … 83)

Betty J. Eadie, similarly Dr Eben Alexander, also experienced a new way of learning when her spirit journeyed to other spheres. Knowledge came from the light, directly in her mind and her questions had been answered before she fully asked them. She was thrilled with the freedom of learning. *"My comprehension was such that I could understand volumes in an instant,"* she writes in her book.

*"Then questions began coming to my mind. I wanted to know why I had died as I had – not prematurely, but how my spirit had come to him before the resurrection. I was still laboring under the teachings and beliefs of my childhood. His light now began to fill my mind, and my questions were answered even before I fully asked them. **His light was knowledge.**" (page 43)*

Betty realized that things had been blocked from her by a 'veil' of forgetfulness at her birth, so now she was very happy to get true knowledge about death and Jesus Christ.

"In my fears, I had misinterpreted death ... The grave was never intended for the spirit – only for the body. I felt no judgment for having been mistaken ...

I understood that he was the Son of God, though he himself was also a god ... His mission was to come into world to teach love. *This knowledge was more like remembering. Things were coming back to me from long before my life on earth, things that had been purposely blocked from me by a 'veil' of forgetfulness at my birth. (page 43 ... 44)*

Betty also got the information that *"Within our universe are both positive and negative energies ... Positive energy is basically just what we would think it is: light, goodness, kindness, love, patience, charity, hope, and so on.*

And negative energy is just what we would think it is: darkness, hatred, fear (Satan's greatest tool), unkindness, intolerance, selfishness, despair ...

If we understood the power of our thoughts, we would guard them more closely. If we understood the awesome power of our words, we would prefer silence to almost anything negative." (page 57 ... 58)

Betty learned that we are given agency to act for ourselves here, on the earth and that God does not intervene in our lives *"unless we asked him."* She was relieved to find that the earth is not our natural home but only a temporary place for our schooling.

"Spiritually, we are at various degrees of light – which is knowledge – *and because of our divine, spiritual nature we are filled with the desire to do good. Our earthly selves, however, are constantly in opposition to our spirits. I saw how weak the flesh is. But it is persistent. Although our spirit bodies are full of light, truth, and love, they must battle constantly to overcome the flesh ... Those who are truly developed will find a perfect harmony between their flesh and spirits." (page 50)*

There is astonishing similarity between Betty's report about the spirit's battling constantly to overcome the flesh and Jesus' teaching about the same issue. It is noteworthy that she had no special philosophical or theological education and she had certainly not read the gnostic gospels either which at that time were not yet published. She asserts that she got her knowledge directly from the source, "the figure of light", i.e. Jesus Christ.

IS OUR "CHIMPANZEE BRAIN" ABLE TO CREATE AND STORE THOUGHTS?

It is said that the following joke is circulating among brain surgeons:

An astronaut just returned from a space trip when he met a friend who was brain surgeon.

"Now I am quite sure that God does not exist! I've been out in space and did not seen him. "

"Well," said the brain surgeon. "I have carried out many brain operations, but I have not seen a single thought. That does not mean that thoughts do not exist."

This simple joke points out the dilemma of scientists researching the "mysteries" of the human brain. For the truth is that, despite all research, no one has so far managed to locate a single thought in the human brain. It is paradoxical that, although all scientific research **is** based on thinking, there is no instrument that can show what a brain surgeon thinks while operating the brain of a patient.

Electroencephalograph (EEG), which is a device used to register general brain activity, can never detect what a patient is thinking on while being examined or operated. The instrument attached to the scalp of the patient by means of electrodes registers only the changes in the electromagnetic waves emitted by the brain and not the thoughts of the examined person.

Béla Balogh, author of the book *The Ultimate Reality* puts the provocative question: *"can we really suppose that brain create thoughts?"* He says that *"The human brain may be extraordinarily complicated, but ultimately it is made up of simple 'terrestrial' materials and is therefore of a relatively low energy level ... Matter, as a set of standing waves, can be described in terms of frequencies falling between those of visible light and high-level gamma radiation. If no higher energy levels or frequencies existed within us, we would be unable to investigate or quantify energies like those of cosmic radiation for the simple reason that we would be unable to postulate their existence."*

Soviet researchers who assumed that thoughts were electromagnetic waves produced by the brain carrying information, carefully checked this hypothesis under the leadership of a physiologist, Leonid Vasiliev in the 1930's.

"In this experiment they worked with three subjects, who they managed to make fall asleep hypnotically by telepathic suggestion. They also managed to undo the hypnosis with the help of telepathic commands. After this 'hypnogenic' method had been successful in a number of cases, both the transmitter and the receiver were locked up in a lead chamber, whose function was to obstruct the assumed electromagnetic waves similarly to a Faraday-cage. To their greatest surprise the experiments did not stop being successful" (Quotation taken from Béla Balogh's book, The Ultimate Reality).

The Russian researchers were surprised when seeing that the thought of the transmitter, who actually was in Sevastopol, was capable to get through the walls of a lead chamber, then travel a distance of 1700 km until it was picked up by a receiver in Leningrad.

Lead chambers are actually used to protect people and objects from high-energy radiation. The fact that thought could penetrate walls similar to a lead chamber, led the researcher give up the hypothesis that thoughts are generated of a matter-brain consisting of low-frequency electromagnetic waves.

Researchers have tried to evaluate each segment of the electromagnetic spectra they know, hoping to find the frequency to which thought belongs. As no final, plausible result has yet been reached in this field, it is supposed that thought exists somewhere beyond the known electromagnetic spectrum. Doctors and brain researchers use careful words and expressions like "maybe", "possibly", "probably", or "we cannot draw any definite conclusions. However, there are humble and straightforward scientists who simply admit the shortages of medical researches. One of them is Professor Lars Olsson, neuro-biologist at Karolinska University in Stockholm who says:

"Our methods we used in examining the structure, biochemistry and activity of the brain were quite rudimentary. It could be compared to a radio. Imagine that you are holding a radio in your hands for the first time and you are trying to examine it as we do with the brain. A biochemist would break it into pieces and grind it into powder to establish the amount of copper, iron, aluminum, silicon, plaster, etc. it contains. A physiologist would push an electrode that is as thick as a telephone-post into it and would examine electromagnetic disturbances. I am a histologist, that is a researcher of tissues. I would perhaps fill the radio with paraffin and would slice it into one micrometer streaks that I would examine them with the help of a microscope. We would certainly learn a lot as a result of the co-operation, but we would hardly understand that the radio actually receives the information from outside in form of waves and transforms them into speech and music." (A Book on the Brain-32 Swedish Researchers on the Brain and its Diseases, 1995/This quotation is taken from Béla Balogh's book, The Ultimate Reality)

Scientists who measure electromagnetic waves and levels of energy in the human brain, reject paranormal phenomena by saying that they have no explanation for their occurrence. Physicists and psychologists, who have tried to find out the mystery of the special abilities of mediums, have not yet either been able to answer the question: from where do these persons get the information about things they should not know? The case of Edgar Cayce, for example, perplexed doctors, scientists and psychologists. How could he, who actually had attended school for only six years, without having any medical education, bring about more than 6 000 precise diagnoses, in many cases even suggesting the right treatment of the patient without meeting the patient personally? He was provided with only the name and address of the person, who lived several hundreds or thousands of kilometers away.

Scientists and brain researchers in Western countries still believe that the brain controls consciousness while some Far-eastern yogis, who are able to suspend their life functions often for days on end, or slow them down to an extraordinary degree, maintain that consciousness rules the body. These yogis know how to use the high frequency energies that come from "outside" and can be used as "control units" of the material world.

"What is consciousness and where is it localized?" is a question that, besides the one about mind, memory and soul should be answered as it touches the utmost existential question of life and death. If we suppose that thoughts, consciousness and soul are not products of the matter-body but of an "out-of-body control system", then we may hope that our thoughts and feelings "survive" in an out-of-body memory-bank when our physical body dies.

Materialists, who think that it is the brain that forms and stores thoughts, emotions and sensory experiences, believe that there is nothing left of man after death.

However, thanks to intensive research into activities of the brain, there are several scientists who do not agree with the pessimistic opinion of the materialists.

Deepak Chopra, author of the book titled *Life After Death,* was born in India but lives and works as a doctor in the United States. Thanks to his background he combines traditional Western medicine with Eastern view of life. He says that since every cell in our body, including the brain cells, undergo constant chemical changes, it is very likely that the "memory bank" of our thoughts and feelings does not exist in the physical body that is constantly "destroyed and renewed" at the cellular level. Our memory-bank should be localized in a safe, imperishable out-of-body place.

There are about ten billion cells in the average human brain and of these ca 0 to 50 000 neurons die each day. When a person turns 70, about 10% of the person's original neurons are lost. The miracle is that even if a person loses about 25 000 brain cells every day, which means nine million per year, that person is still unlikely to forget her name and address. If all the information we get by learning or experiencing things were indeed stored in perishable brain cells, we should lose them and never remember them again.

   Some scientists say that it may be possible that the brain creates "backup copies", storing the same information in several places and that is why we do not forget things even if brain cells are damaged. However, other scientists contradict this theory by saying that the constant information flow to the brain cells would require a highly developed control program in order to perform the complicated "backup copy" activity. They also say that it is doubtful that a lifeless matter-cell that according to evolution theory, was by chance transformed into living matter, could get through a long process of evolution by chance culminating in the development of complex cell collections called brain that writes programs it needs to maintain itself, to store thoughts and feelings and to give consciousness to itself.

If the brain does not create nor store thoughts, what function does it have then? Béla Balogh and several brain researchers suppose that the brain may have a kind of "broadcasting" task similar to a radio that is both a receiver and transmitter of information that comes from an external source. As there must be a constant interplay between the receiver and the external sender, there should be a "memory-bank" beyond the perishable matter-brain where all information is stored when brain cells die.

Research on near-death experiences also indicates that each person has an out of body "memory-bank", in religious contexts often called The Book of Life, that stores information on what one has done and experienced during the earthly life. Raymond A. Moody and other researchers of near-death experience report that people who did a journey on the other side, could see a review of their life. They did not only see the events but they even experienced the immediate emotional impact of their deeds. They could feel the grief and the pain caused to another person when acting badly, but they also could feel happiness when helping and being kind to a person. They learned and concluded that love is the most important in life.

Before his near-death experience Doctor Eben Alexander as a neurosurgeon had a scientific view of what brain, consciousness and memory is. He considered the brain to be "a highly delicate, electrically charged machine" that produces the phenomenon of consciousness and that can "be fixed" when it is damaged. We read in his book titled *Proof of Heaven:*

"As much as I'd grown up wanting to believe in God and Heaven and an afterlife, my decades in the rigorous scientific world of academic neurosurgery had profoundly called into question how such things could exist. Modern neuroscience dictates that the brain gives rise to consciousness — to the mind, to the soul, to the spirit, to whatever you choose to call that invisible, intangible part of us that truly makes us who we are — and I had little doubt that it was correct ... over the years my scientific worldview gently but steadily undermined my ability to believe in something larger", he relates. *(Eben Alexander: Proof of Heaven, page 34 ... 35)*

After his near-death experience he totally changed his opinion and said:

"We — the spiritual beings currently inhabiting our evolutionarily developed mortal brains and bodies, the product of the earth and the exigencies of the earth — make the real choices. True thought is not the brain's affair ...

True thought is pre-physical. This is the thinking-behind-the thinking ... A thinking that is not dependent on linear deduction, but that moves fast as lightning, making connections on different levels, bringing them together. In the face of this free, inner intelligence, our ordinary thought is hopelessly slow and fumbling. ... The subliminal thinking that is always there, when we really need it, but that we have all too often lost the ability both to access and to believe in ...

To experience thinking outside the brain is to enter a world of instantaneous connections that make ordinary thinking (i.e. those aspects limited by physical brain and the speed of light) seem like some hopelessly sleepy and plodding event." (page 84 ... 85)

Jesus, Betty J. Eddie and Dr Alexander talk about a filter, in religious context about a veil, or even a form of spiritual blindness that blocks our access to knowledge about other dimensions of universe. We read in Dr. Alexander's book:

"Just as our brains work hard every moment of our waking lives to filter out the barrage of sensory information coming at us from our physical surroundings, selecting the material we actually need in order to survive, so it is that forgetting our trans-earthly identities also allows us to be 'here and now' far more effectively ... ... If we knew too much of the spiritual realm now, then navigating our lives on earth would be an even greater challenge than it already is." (page 81)

PADRE PIO AND "THE BOOK OF LIFE"

The special ability of mediums to give information of events that occurred in the past or will occur in the future life of a person whom the medium never met before, proves that the "brain filter" of some persons can be partly removed or opened for a while, helping mediums to get access to the Book of Life /memory-bank of unknown people. Padre Pio had this ability besides his capacity of bilocation and healing. He possessed the charisma of seeing distant things in a person's life, as well as to view the future. People who came to Padre Pio to confess, were surprised when after a few minutes talking to the friar, he was able to mention the most secret events of their lives, sometimes even admonishing them because of the "sins" they had committed. Many people got scared and angry at first, but later they came back to the prior with repentance.

The story of a man, who had the reputation of being a good Catholic, witnesses about Padre Pio's ability of revealing secrets of a person's life.

"A certain man who had the reputation of being a good Catholic, was admired and esteemed by all who knew him. Actually he was living in sin. He had divorced his wife and had relationship with another woman. On one occasion he went to confession to Padre Pio. In order to justify himself, he started talking about his 'spiritual crisis'. ... Padre Pio jumped up at once and shouted, 'What spiritual crisis? You are a litterbug! And God is angry with you. Go away!" (padrepio.catholicwebservices.com: Supernatural knowledge)

Alberto Del Fante, a lawyer and journalist, was an intellectual freethinker who had been irritated by the articles in newspapers reporting about the "supernatural abilities" of Padre Pio. Without investigating if the reports were true or not, he accused Padre Pio to be a liar, a charlatan and an imposter, who profited from people's ignorance and credulity. But later, an event in his family brought him closer to Padre Pio.

A dear family member got very sick, so Alberto's family and friends were very sad and desperate. One of the friends, without informing the family, asked Padre Pio for help, after which the deadly sick person recovered within 24 hours, to the doctors' amazement.

After this miracle, Del Fante, the skeptic journalist, decided to travel to San Giovanni Rotondo in order to find out if Padre Pio really was a "miracle worker" or an impostor.

When he arrived to the church in San Giovanni Rotondo, he wanted to get as close as possible to Padre Pio, so he decided to go to confession.

"I went to confession … without enthusiasm, without faith. I thought that he was only an ordinary priest," Del Fante related later. *"However he differed from other priests in one way: he knew everything. He told me that I had belonged to a society that accept God but dislike his priests.- Probably he guessed that I was a Freemason member, … we discussed a little philosophy and talked about people who – although they lacked faith – let themselves be guided by their conscience …*

– Padre, I said, my deeds have always been honest and if it sometimes happened that the animal in me tried to overpower me, my conscience said: do not do that, do this. I've never been a believer, but I have always been honest.

– What? Honest? Also the time … or the time …

He told me things that he in no way ought to know. (Ursula Ljungren: Padre Pio)

Padre Pio astonished Del Fante who later became a close friend and spiritual "child" of the friar. The journalist stopped writing *against* the father and instead started to report *about* all the marvelous events happening around him. Del Fantes' reports resulted in his writing three books about Padre Pio.

Padre Pio's ability to view the future and tell about distant things is documented in many scripts. The friar who was the Guardian of the convent of St. Giovanni Rotondo reported the following story:

"Last year a dealer from Pisa came to Padre Pio for a healing of his daughter. Fra Pio looked at him and said: 'You are sicker than your daughter.' 'No, no, no Padre, I'm very well!', said the man. 'Wretch!,' Padre Pio shouted. 'Unfortunate! How can you feel well with so many sins on your conscience? I can see at least thirty-two sins!'

The dealer was perplexed. After his confession, he said to everybody who listened about his meeting Padre Pio: 'He could tell me everything about my life! He knew everything!'" (padrepio.catholicwebservices.com: Supernatural knowledge)

Padre Pio's ability to reveal the secrets of a persons' life reminds us that Jesus had the same ability. We read in The Gospel of John, Chapter 4 that Jesus met a Samaritan woman at Jacob's well and said to her:

'Go, call your husband, and come here.'

The woman answered and said, 'I have no husband.' Jesus said to her, 'You have well said, – I have no husband – for you have had five husbands, and the one whom you now have is not your husband; in that you spoke truly.'

The woman said to him, 'Sir, I perceive that you are a prophet.'

The woman then left her water-pot, went her way into the city, and said to the men,

'Come, see a man who told me all things that I ever did.' (John 4:16 ... 29)

Padre Pio' ability to predict events also surprised people. A woman from Bologna (Italy) has told the following story about her mother who once went to Padre Pio with some friends:

"Once my mother went to father Pio with some of her friends. She met Father Pio in the sacristy of the convent of San Giovanni Rotondo ... Padre Pio told her: 'Why are you here? Go home, your husband is sick'. My mother thought she had left her husband in good condition. Anyway, she turned back by the first available train. When she arrived home she asked about my father's health. There was no news. But during the night my father had serious respiratory difficulties. Something pressed him in the throat ...

The surgeon who later operated him, removed at least two basins of pus from his throat". (padrepio.catholicwebservices.com: Supernatural knowledge)

Padre Carmelo, Superior of the Convent of St. Giovanni Rotondo, also witnesses about the prophetic spirit of Padre Pio:

"During the last World War, every day we talked about the war and about the military victories of Germany. One morning I was in the little parlor of the convent and was reading the news about the German troops moving in the direction of Moscow. For me, this was important news as it meant that the war would end with the final victory of Germany. When I left the parlor, I met Padre Pio in the corridor and gladly told him the news: 'Father , the war is ended! Germany has won!'- 'Who has told you that?, Padre Pio asked. 'The newspaper, Father!' I answered. Padre Pio asked: 'Has Germany won the war? Keep in your mind that Germany, this time, will lose the war, worse than the last time! Remember this!'. I said: 'Father, the Germans are already near Moscow.' He added: 'Remember what I have told you!' – I said: 'But, if Germany loses the war, Italy will lose the war as well!' – But he said emphatically: 'We will see if they will end the war together.'

I didn't understand those words, taking into account the alliance of Italy and Germany, but his words became clear for me after the armistice of Italy with England and America 1943, 8th of September and when Italy started war against Germany."

(padrepio.catholicwebservices.com: Supernatural knowledge)

It was not only living people who wanted to contact Padre Pio to ask for help but even souls from the other side. The friar was often perplexed and confused of such apparitions and at the beginning he did not know how to handle his ability of being a medium.

"One evening Padre Pio was in a room on the ground floor of the convent, turned to a guestroom. He was alone and had just laid down on the cot, when, suddenly, a man, wound in a black mantle, appeared to him. Padre Pio was surprised and arose to ask the man who he was and what he wanted ... 'I am Pietro Di Mauro,' he said. 'I died in a fire in this convent, on September 18, 1908. In fact this convent, after the expropriation of the ecclesiastical goods, had been turned into a hospice for elderly. I died in the flames, while I was sleeping on my straw mattress, right in this room. I have come from Purgatory: and ask you to celebrate Mass for me tomorrow morning. Thanks to one Mass I will be able to enter into Paradise.' Father Pio promised the man to have Mass for him."

Even if Padre Pio realized that he was talking to a dead person, he wanted to accompany him to the door of the convent; when they were outside, the man suddenly disappeared.

Padre Pio looked quite frightened when he re-entered the convent. Padre Paolino of Casacalenda, Superior of the convent, noticed his nervousness and asked what the problem was. Padre Pio told him about his experience and asked for permission to celebrate Holy Mass for the deceased soul.

"A few days later, Father Paolino, wanting to verify the information, went to the office of the registry of the commune of St. Giovanni Rotondo. He asked for permission to consult the register of the deceased persons in the year 1908."

Father Paolino found the following registered information: *"On September 18, 1908 Pietro Di Mauro died in the fire of the hospice."* (padrepio.catholicwebservices.com: The Apparitions)

If somebody asked Padre Pio about his abilities, he generally said: "It is from God. I do what I have to do."

Already in his childhood he had apparitions of Angels, of Jesus and of the Madonna, but sometimes also of demons; he did not mention anything about the visions as he believed that they were normal and happen to all people. Later, as a friar, though happy with his abilities, he was sometimes scared and felt physically exhausted and sick when energies of higher frequency level struck him. He writes about this in a letter addressed to his spiritual director Padre Benedetto describing his experience of being transverberated.

Transverberation has often been referred to as "the mystical wound of love" or the "assault of an angel or a seraph". When such a celestial being appears, the visited person feels the heart or the side being pierced with a lance or sword. This may sound science fiction but the truth is that there are many stories of transverberation in different religious contexts.

Padre Pio received the internal and external mark of the transverberation on August 5, 1918 when he was thirty-one years old. Sixteen days later he described the experience in a letter written to Padre Benedetto:

"By virtue of obedience, I have decided to reveal to you what happened to me on the evening of the fifth and for the entire day of the sixth of this month ...

while I was hearing a boy's confession ... I was suddenly horrified by the sight of a celestial being ... He had in his hand a sort of weapon like a very long, sharp steel blade which seemed to emit fire. At the very moment I got this vision, I saw the being hurling the weapon into my soul. I cried out as I could and felt I was dying ... My agony lasted uninterruptedly until the morning of the seventh August. I suffered of anguish but even my internal organs were torn and ruptured by the weapon. From that day on I have been mortally wounded. I feel in the depth of my soul a wound that is always open and it causes me continual agony." (Letter 1) (www.padrepio.catholicwebservices.com)

The event Padre Pio describes in this letter should not be interpreted metaphorically but considered as a real experience as he really had been physically wounded. The wound he got in his side was bleeding for the rest of his life and caused him much pain. After being wounded by that celestial being, he had to stay in bed for three days as he felt pain and weakness and the side wound caused him intense suffering later too. He wrote to Padre Benedetto:

"The heart wound bleeds continually, especially from Thursday evening until Saturday. Dear Father, I am dying of pain because of the wounds and the embarrassment I feel deep in my soul. I am afraid I shall bleed to death if the Lord does not hear my heartfelt supplication to relieve me of this condition." (Letter 1 – www.padrepio.catholicwebservices.com)

One year later, on January 29. 1919 he writes to Padre Benedetto:
"Dear Father, I feel I am drowned in the immense ocean of the love of my Beloved ... My small heart is incapable of containing this immense love. It is true that it is inside and outside me. But, dear God, when You pour Yourself into the little vessel of my being, I suffer the agony of not being able to contain You. You have vanquished me; You have burned my insides; You have placed a river of fire within me." (Letters 1 – www.padrepio.catholicwebservices.com)

When Padre Pio describes his spiritual and physical state by using phrases such as "river of fire" or "ocean of fire" that burns his insides, he is actually talking about a power coming from dimensions with higher energy frequency levels than we, humans are used to. When the "protecting filter", called "the veil" in religious context, existing between our world and other dimensions is removed for a while, the person experiencing it, feels "wounded" and "burned" by the power and energy of that other world. Although Padre Pio suffered because of the incompatibility of the energies working at different frequency levels in his body, he felt happy about the abilities the higher powers entrusted him with.

To better understand how these powers worked in and through Padre Pio, it is noteworthy to recall that the friar experienced extremely high fever at various times throughout his life. When his fever reached 45–46 degrees Celsius for example, the thermometer broke into pieces. His doctors were never able to find a medical explanation regarding his high fever or his being suddenly deadly sick for a few days and then quickly recovering after two or three days.

All this has remained a mystery, like so many other aspects of his life.

All information about Padre Pio's ability of healing people by using the power he was given by the invisible world, reminds us of Jesus' healing a woman "having a flow of blood for twelve years". When she was healed by only touching his garment, Jesus perceived power going out from him. We read in the Gospel of Luke:

"Now a woman, having a flow of blood for twelve years, who had spent all her livelihood on physicians and could not be healed by any, came from behind and touched the border of his garment. And immediately her flow of blood stopped.

And Jesus said, 'Who touched me? 'When all denied it, Peter and those with him said, 'Master, the multitudes throng you and press you, and you say, 'Who touched me?'

But Jesus said, 'Somebody touched me, for I perceived power going out from me.'" (Luke 8:43–46)

Jesus' ability of healing the sick, or "raising the dead" has been questioned for nearly 2000 years. Many theologians interpret the stories symbolically and scientists consider them to be fabricated stories that satisfy the religious individuals' need to believe in the supernatural. They doubt that either Padre Pio, or Jesus or any other people with paranormal abilities work with energies and powers they get from another dimension of reality.

According to several Nag Hammadi scriptures, Jesus talked about the necessity of being "filled" with the power of spirit. When teaching the disciples how to protect themselves against the power of the demon, he said:

"So, I tell you, be filled and leave no space within you empty, or he who is coming will mock you," he says.

> "Then Peter answered, 'Look, three times you have told us, *Be filled,* but we are filled.'
> The Savior said, 'For this reason I have told you, **Be filled**, that you may not lack ... To be filled is good and to lack is bad. ... whoever is filled also lacks ... Be filled with spirit but lack in reason, for reason is of the soul. It is soul." (NH, The Secret Book of James, page 24 ... 25)

In modern times when nuclear physicists are searching for energies at different frequency levels, more research should be done concerning the powers and energies of persons possessing paranormal abilities.

Astrophysicists, who work hard to get information about planets, galaxy and other mysteries of the universe, never think that Jesus has given loads of information about the spheres as well as about the mysterious light and darkness existing in different dimensions. He said:

"I have come as a light into the world, that whoever believes in me should not abide in darkness," (John 13:46)

THE SUPREME BEING IS THE ONE GENERATOR OF ALL RADIANCE AND VIBRATION

The Gospel of John in the New Testament as well as the gnostic gospels found in Nag Hammadi attest that talking about the eternal Light was one of the central issues of Jesus. Even the prayers he used witness about his attachment to the eternal Light of the One, the Supreme Being of universe. The different translations and interpretations of the so called "original Aramaic Lord's Prayer" show that the invocation of the Shimmering Light of All was very important also for the early Christians. Here are some versions of prayers in which eternal Light is invoked:

The Lord's Prayer translated from Aramaic by John Marc Hammer Below:

Father-Mother of the Cosmos, **Shimmering Light of All**
Focus Your Light Within us*, As we breathe Your Holy Breath.*
Enter the sanctuary of our hearts,
Uniting within us the sacred rays of Your Power and Beauty
Let Your Heart's desire **Unite heaven and earth** *Through our sacred union On earth, as it is in heaven …*

The Lord's Prayer translated and interpreted from Aramaic:

*Oh Thou, from whom the breath of life comes, **who fills all realms of sound, light and vibration, May Your light be experienced in my utmost holiest**. Your Heavenly Domain approaches. Let Your will come true- in the universe (all that vibrates) just as on earth (that is material and dense). Give us wisdom (understanding, assistance) for our daily need, detach the fetters of faults that bind us, (karma) like we let go the guilt of others. Let us not be lost in superficial things (materialism, common temptations), but let us be freed from that what keeps us off from our true purpose.*

   From You comes the all-working will, the lively strength to act, the song that beautifies all and renews itself from age to age.

   Sealed in trust, faith and truth, (I confirm with my entire being) (Amen)

The Lord's Prayer according to another interpretation of the original Aramaic prayer:

*Oh Thou who are the creator (generator) of all radiance and vibration **Soften the matter of our being and find a place within us where your Presence can abide. **Fill us with your power** so that we may be empowered to bear the fruit of our mission Let each of our actions bear fruit in accordance with your desire **Endow us with wisdom** to produce and share what each being needs to grow and flourish. **Untie the tangled threads of destiny that bind us**, as we release others from the entanglement of past mistakes. **Do not let us be seduced by that which would divert us from our true purpose**, but illuminate the opportunities of the present moment.*

   For you are the cause, the fruitful vision, the birth, the power and fulfillment, as all will be united and made Whole once again.

The Lord's Prayer, based on the Syriac Peshitta, interpreted and authorized by theologians and ecclesiastics of the international institutional Christian church:

Our Father, who art in heaven, **hollowed be thy Name***, thy kingdom come, thy will be done, on earth as it is in heaven. Give us this day our daily bread. And* ***forgive us our trespasses****, as we forgive those who trespass against us, And* **lead us not into temptation,** *but deliver us from evil. For thine is the kingdom, and the power, and the glory, for ever and ever. Amen*

The **Lord's Prayer** is a powerful prayer used by all the Christians in the world in the version and interpretation the institutional church has authorized. Christian members of the institutional churches believe that the Lord's Prayer they pray is the original one, and they do not know that there are more versions prayed by Christians with different backgrounds, experiences and knowledge.

Comparing the translations and interpretations, we see that the version authorized by the institutional church differs mostly. Only in this version the invocation of the eternal Light is totally omitted from the prayer. Only in this version the name of God is hollowed. As no name is indicated, one may wonder "which name "should be hollowed? Jahve, Sebaoth, El-Eleth or Adonai are names used by the Jews but not by Jesus. According to scripts found in Nag Hammadi, he used the term The One when teaching about God, and he actually even said that **The One has no name**:

"**The One Who Is** *is immortal and eternal, and being eternal, is without birth, for whoever is born will die; unconceived, without a beginning, for whoever has a beginning has an end; undominated,* **without a name***, for whoever has a name has been made by another;* **unnamable***, with no human form, for whoever has a human form has been made by another. The One Who is has an appearance of its own, …" (NH, The Wisdom of Jesus Christ: 93,24 … 95,18, page 288 … 289)*

Christians using The Lord's Prayer interpreted by the institutional church asks God not to *lead us into temptation* without considering that, according to Jesus' teaching, the tempter is Satan and not God. The peculiar sentence "Lead us not into temptation" should be considered as a bad interpretation or translation of an Arameic prayer or as a personal wording about God of Israel. Unfortunately, Christian theologians have never questioned or reinterpreted this phrase.

The different traditions of the Lord's Prayer indicate the different images of God too. The members of the institutional church ask for forgiveness of the trespasses as they believe in God, the king who judges and punishes people at the end of the times. Besides, the God they pray to is far away, in the heaven and wants the Christians to surrender totally.

Other Christian groups pray to the Father-Mother of the Cosmos, the Shimmering Light of All, or to the creator (generator) of all radiance and vibration. They are confidant and ask for help to become better spiritual beings and to be filled with Light and power. They use sentences like: "Focus Your Light Within us"; "Uniting within us the sacred rays of Your Power", or "Fill us with Your power". They do not think of God as a tempter, but they pray for "not to be lost in superficial things", and "to be freed from that what keeps from true purpose".

Talking about the celestial light is a recurrent phenomenon not only in Jesus' discourses or in the prayers of the early Christians, but also in the reports of paranormal experiences, may it be a near-death experience or the visit of a celestial being.

In the Acts we read about the Pharisee Saul (later called Paul) who experienced the Light that changed his life and faith totally. He was on his way to Damascus where he would continue imprisoning and torturing Christians when *"suddenly a light shone around him from heaven. Then he fell to the ground, and heard a voice saying to him, 'Saul, Saul, why are you persecuting me?' And he said, 'Who are you, Lord?' And the Lord said: 'I am Jesus, whom you are persecuting.'" (Acts 9:3–5)*

This experience had a great impact on Saul (Paul), who *"was three days without sight, and neither ate nor drank."* …*"And when he had received food, he was strengthened. Then Saul spent some days with the disciples in Damascus. Immediately he preached the Christ in the synagogues, that Jesus is the Son of God …*

Now after many days were past, the Jews plotted to kill him." (Acts 9:9 … 23)

Scientists say that all living cells of plants, animals and human beings emit biophotons, i.e. energy emitting light which cannot be seen by the naked eye but can be measured with the help of special equipment. The light emission of the cells is an expression of the functional state of the cells.

The discovery of light emission of the cells is a rather new breakthrough for doctors in Western countries, but it has been a known phenomenon in China, India and other Eastern countries. The Traditional Chinese Medicine has used for thousands of years for healing purpose the "chi" which is the energy flowing in the meridians of our body. Thanks to the light emitted by the "chi", the energy meridians have been traced and have been used for healing by acupuncture. According to Indian Yoga physiology, "prana" is the light and energy of the regulating force of the cells.

When we read about **the light as a revelation phenomenon** we should remember that nuclear physicians are also fascinated of the mystery of the light at a subatomic level. They talk for instance about the dualism of the light that means that light can behave like a stream of particles (called photons) exhibiting at the same time wave-like properties. They also talk about a hypothetical particle that moves faster than the light we know, and that may be called a super-luminous-particle.

While scientists do complicated and expensive experiments using sophisticated terminologies and theories concerning the mysteries of light, God The One lets humans in different life situations to experience the eternal Light.

Gunnar Hillerdal, a Swedish professor who has researched paranormal experiences, reports in his book *God Reveals Himself – (Så ger sig Gud till känna),* the story of a woman who had an out of-body experience while she was lying in her bed and was reading a book:

"*One night I was lying and reading a book … I felt unusually harmonious and filled with gratitude …*

Suddenly I found myself in another state. I was no longer aware that I was reading, and I was not aware of my body or of the room. I was not aware of my ordinary existence either.

I felt like floating in a sea that constantly was in motion. I followed with a steady harmonic stream and felt my unification with the whole creation. My first thought was: 'Is it that simple?' … I looked up and saw **a great source of light**. *The bright light mingled with the darkness. I felt like being at the beginning of creation … I was one with the whole.*

I floated forward in the stream of darkness and light. Then I was back in my bed again and was surprised by my experience." (G. Hillerdal, page 25 f)

An early morning in August 2005, I myself experienced the eternal Light which is brighter than any light in our material world.

While I was lying half-awake in my bed, I suddenly left my body. Next moment I was standing in the middle of a large and very bright room with walls of crystal-ceramics. I saw that crystalline water was flowing down the walls of the room which was filled with a light that was brighter than any light I have ever seen.

I was little scared as the water was raising and filling the room. "I will be drowned" I thought while standing in the middle of the room totally filled with water. But my fear disappeared when I unexpectedly felt that the water and the bright light was flushing every cell of my body and my soul. I physically felt the cleaning effect of the flushing water and of the bright light.

Then the water was running in a strange way upwards the walls and the room was emptied. After a short time I was back in my bed perplexed by my experience which has helped me later to better understand the meaning of baptism and the dialogue between Jesus and Nicodemus. We read in The Gospel of John:

"There was a man of the Pharisees named Nicodemus, a ruler of the Jews.

This man came to Jesus by night and said to him, 'Rabbi, we know that you are a teacher come from God; for no one can do these signs that you do unless God is with him.'

Jesus answered and said to him, 'Most assuredly; I say to you, unless one is born again, he cannot see the kingdom of God.'

Nicodemus said to him, 'How can a man be born when he is old? Can he enter a second time into his mother's womb and be born?'

Jesus answered, 'Most assuredly, I say to you, unless one is born of water and the Spirit, he cannot enter the kingdom of God.

That which is born of the flesh is flesh, and that which is born of the Spirit is spirit.

Do not marvel that I said to you, 'You must be born again.'" (John 3:1–7)

The mystery of the unknown reality has always fascinated man, especially when one experiences events that have no scientific or logical explanation. **Carl Jung,** renowned psychiatrist and originator of a new psychology, declared spirit as a living force at the center of the psyche. Born in Basel, Switzerland in 1875, Carl Jung was influenced by his father, a church pastor who had lost his faith, and by his mother, who was an intuitive woman to whom mysterious events seemed to happen. At one occasion, for instance, a solid oak table in front of her emitted a sound like a gunshot and split in the middle.

Paranormal events experienced by his family members as well as by Jung himself generated his first inquiries into life's deeper realities. He claimed that *"Man's psyche is as infinite within as the universe is without."* His letters, seminars and the autobiographical work *"Memories, Dreams, Reflections",* as well as his *Collected Works* provide a wide overview of his experiences and ideas.

Jung had so many visions and paranormal experiences that at first he feared he might be going mad. Finally he realized that he had to explore his inner landscape, the inner depths and heights of his soul. Curious about the supernatural, about life after death as well as about the human soul, he was drawn to study and work with psychiatry that was a new science at that time.

One night, in the second half of his life, C. Jung woke and saw a greenish gold figure of the crucified Christ "marvelously beautiful" hovering over him, bathing in bright light. This apparition had a great impact on Carl. As a scientist, he wanted to grasp the meaning of his vision, which he interpreted as a symbol of the union of spirit and matter in human flash.

At the age of sixty-nine (1944) C. Jung suffered a heart attack and found himself floating in space and seeing the Earth that "bathed in blue light …". It was "the most glorious thing I had ever seen", Jung wrote about his out-of-body experience. He landed on a black meteorite where he met a black Hindu who was sitting silently in lotus posture on a stone bench before the entrance of a temple. Jung later wrote, in *Memories, Dreams, Reflections*: *'I had the certainty I was about to enter an illumined room and … I would at last … know what had been before me, why I had come into being and where my life was flowing.' But before he could enter, he saw his doctor rise up as a spirit from the earth, framed 'by a golden laurel wreath.' He had been sent to bring Carl back. The next instant, Jung found himself back in his body, sick at heart.*

During his weeks of recovery, Carl experienced a series of exalted visions: 'These were states of ineffable joy. Angels were present, and light … Night after night I floated in a state of purest bliss, thronged round with images of all creation? At this point the most productive period of his lifework began." (Dan Millman & Doug Childers: Bridge Between Worlds, page 124) At this point C. Jung also experiences a kind of *"affirmation of things as they are: an unconditional 'yes' to that which is … acceptance of the conditions of existence … of my own nature." (Memories, Dreams, Reflections)*

The immensity of supernatural experiences, reported in books and collected in documents, suggests that miracles do not happen in laboratories where scientists do their research, but they happen in real life unexpectedly, overwhelming people.

Andy Lakey was greeting New Year 1986 in a friend's apartment upstairs from his own, when he suddenly felt his heart palpitating rapidly, and felt extremely ill." I felt certain I was going to die," he said later. He somehow stumbled downstairs to his apartment and got into the shower fully clothed. He turned on the cold water, hoping it might revive him and prayed for the first time since he was eight years old. "*I still remember the prayer,*" he reported. "*I said, 'God is good. God is great. God, if you let me live, I will never do drugs again. I will also do something to help humankind.*" Andy further reported:

"*Almost instantly, I felt a twirling sensation, like a little tornado or whirlpool around my feet … there were seven figures, and as they twirled up toward my knees, my thighs, my waist and up to my chest, the twirling got faster and faster … When they reached by heart, they came together as one and put their arms around me … now there was only one figure … It embraced and lifted me into another dimension. There were a thousand planets with ten thousand poles of light extending through them and into … a galaxy of brightness … Every pole was filled with millions of souls in perfect columns and perfect harmony. But I could not get into a pole.*"*(Dan Millman & Doug Childers: Bridge Between Worlds, page 127)*

Andy's friends who had found him unconscious in the shower, brought him to the hospital just in time, and Andy woke up in the emergency room. The doctor told him that due to the massive amount of cocaine in his body, he got a heart-attack.

After this experience, Andy was determined to change his life. He became completely free from his drug addiction and found a new job. He began to contemplate the meaning of his vision that he first illustrated by drawing and then painting it. He was so obsessed of this project that on his thirtieth birthday he decided to quit work and to become a full-time artist. Without bothering that he had never learned how to paint, he created a studio and bought five thousand dollars' worth of supplies and became a full-time artist.

One morning some time later, he went to his studio and began to pray while sitting before one of his paintings.

When he raised his head, **he saw a ball of light** *come through the wall and enter his forehead:*

'*The ball enveloped my body, filling me with pure love, pure energy ... I found myself communicating with three men. They were definitely my angels ... They had beards, whitish hair, very light in color, very bright ... They were giving me information telepathically, and told me exactly what I was to do: I was to paint 2,000 paintings by the year 2000. These angels would take care of everything ... I knew they would give me my art technique; they would teach me to paint,*' Andy reported later. (Dan Millman & Doug Childers, page 128)

Andy has become a famous artist who is known as the painter of angels. As he uses a highly unique technique by thickly applying the paints, mostly direct from the tubes, his paintings are almost three-dimensional and they are not only visual but tactile also; an art consultant suggested him to create paintings for the blind. Admirers and owners of his work include two presidents, Jimmy Carter and Ronald Reagan, artists, as Ray Charles and Stevie Wonder along with many other people who are deeply impressed by his paintings.

Andy's near-death experience and the apparition of the celestial beings who instructed him to paint has had a great impact on his view of life. He said:

"*When I look up at the night sky, I see the stars totally differently ... they're a reminder of what's really out there. In my heart and spirit I see bright planets and poles of light. I see angles flying through the universe, doing the work of God.*" *(Dan Millman & Doug Childers, page 130)*

There are people who think that Andy's vision was a drug-induced hallucination, however, his transformed life and the unique emergence of his artistic gifts suggest otherwise. Andy is not the only person who has experienced **the paranormal phenomenon of light balls.**

One early morning in May 1986 I was lying in bed and listening to the birds' song coming in through the slightly opened window. While I tried to figure out which birds were singing, I suddenly saw three special light balls flowing in through the opened window. I had not much time left to reflect about the origin of the light balls because through them I got a vision about two future events that should occur in my family. Then the light balls disappeared quickly while I still was lying perplexed of my vision. At breakfast I told my family about my strange experience and the unlucky events that should happen according to the message I had got. They listened skeptically and hoped that the events I saw in the vision, should never happen. Unfortunately, to my astonishment, both events came true after a very short time.

On May 16, 1986 at one o'clock in the afternoon David Young, a former marshal and his wife Doris rolled a shopping cart loaded with gasoline bombs, rifles and handguns into the **Cokeville Elementary School**. *"This is a revolution and I'm taking your school hostage",* he said to the school secretary. David Young and his wife herded 150 children and several teachers into a large classroom and demanded three hundred million dollars from the United States government and a personal phone call from President Ronald Reagan. They did not want to negotiate – they said that they would detonate the bombs if their demand would not be accepted. For nearly two and a half hours, anxious parents and friends and other onlookers waited behind the police lines, hoping and praying for a safe resolution – even a miracle. When they heard the cataclysmic explosion and saw the bright orange fire in the large classroom where the children were, the onlookers thought that nobody had a chance to survive the terror action. At that moment they did not know that **a real miracle** was happening in the town of Cokeville. All the hostages survived and none of the injuries were life threatening. Thirty-two people received second-degree burns to their face, and one child was hit by a bullet. *"I can't begin to tell you how lucky they were,"* said Richard Haskell, bomb expert of the Sweeter County Sheriff's Department. *"When you look in that classroom – when you see all that charred furniture and burnt walls – it's amazing that there weren't 150 kids lying in there dead. To call it a miracle would be the understatement of the century." (Dan Millman & Doug Childers: Bridge Between Worlds, page 150)*

This miracle was fully revealed when children began to report to their parents, rescue workers, and police that **"beings of light" who had come "down through the ceiling"**, had helped them. *"Rachel and Katie Walker said they were 'bright like light bulbs, 'and that one hovered over each of the hostages. The angel hovering over Nathan told him she was his great grandmother, and warned him, 'The bomb is going to explode and the two bad people are going to die. 'She then told him, 'Go stand near the window.' Katie's brother Travis heard a clear voice tell him to take his sisters to the window and keep them there, and that they would be all right." (Dan Millman & Doug Childers: Bridge Between Worlds, page 150)*

Many people argue against miracles by saying: "Prove it!", "I have never experienced any" or "I believe only in what I can see, touch or experience". However, these arguments are questionable, as we are supposed to believe in many things that we never can prove, see, touch or experience. Nobody has for instance proved, seen or experienced the creation of humans by evolution as Darwin formulated it and nobody has experienced the BIG BANG. Even if the stories about miracles and paranormal phenomena do not give final answers to the larger questions of life, they may inspire hope and remind us of a mysterious power existing in and outside us.

COLLECTIVE EXPERIENCE OF PARANORMAL PHENOMENA

Madonna Apparitions in Fatima and Zeitoun

Skeptics easily dismiss individual supernatural experiences classifying them as hallucinations, but the "hallucination argument" is not enough when thousands of people report about a collective experience, as for instance the Madonna Apparitions in Fatima (Portugal) and in Zeitoun (Egypt).

In 1915, Lucia Santos, an eight-year-old shepherd girl from Fatima, Portugal, was tending the flock in Cova da Iria when a human form shimmering within a luminous cloud appeared to her. Her report of the apparition was dismissed as stirrings of a young girl's imagination. The apparition visited Lucia three more times that year, and the following year the same shining form appeared to Lucia and to her two young cousins, Francisco and Jacinta Marto. The children reported that it was a beautiful young man who appeared in a sphere of white light and that he presented himself as *"the Angel of Peace,"* and taught them a prayer. The following autumn, he appeared again and administered Communion before departing. Each time, the apparition had great impact on the children, who fell into a deep, trance-like state when they were visited by the so called Angel of Peace. At the beginning the children kept these visits a secret as they were afraid of being accused as liars.

In 1917 when the children reported about the apparition of a Lady whom they saw in a cocoon of light, the local police threatened Lucia to be punished if she does not stop talking about such apparitions. But in 1917, the miracle in Cova da Iria (Fatima) became a series of mass events that transformed the lives of nearly one hundred thousand people.

On May 13 1917, the three shepherd children tending the flock saw a sudden **flash of brilliant white light.** When they walked toward it, **they saw a bright, glowing sphere, in the midst of which stood a tiny woman.** She talked to them and said that she came from heaven, and asked them to return to the same place each month on the same day thereafter.

A month later on June 13, the children were there as the Lady requested. This time fifty people accompanied them and witnessed that the faces of the children were transfigured with unearthly light while they were talking to the Lady of Light. The meeting ended with a loud explosion when a small cloud of light, visible to all, rose above the tree where the children knelt.

The following month, on August 13, 1917 the children were absent, as they were confined by a skeptical official who put them in jail and pressured them to recant their story of the Madonna's miraculous appearances, or else tell him the secrets she had revealed. When they refused to talk to him, he separated them and told each that the others had been killed for refusing to talk. Meanwhile, the crowd gathered in Cova da Iria, and waiting for the apparition, heard a loud thunderclap and saw a luminous cloud that evaporated like mist. The sun shone through the clouds that turned the color of rainbow light. Strange petals fell from the sky, vanishing before they touched the ground.

When the children were released from the prison, they kept going to the place in Cova da Iria indicated by the Madonna. *"The children revealed several prophecies made by the lady in the cloud, all of which came true. She told them that the present war would soon end – World War I ended a year later – but added, 'If people do not stop offending God, another, worse war will begin during the reign of Pius XI'*, said the Lady to the children. *"World War II began in 1939, the last year of Pope Pius' reign. The lady also told the children, 'If Russia is not converted, she will spread her errors throughout the world.' All these prophecies are documented in records made that same year." (Dan Millman & Doug Childers: Bridge Between Worlds, page 36)*

On September 13, a crowd of about thirty thousand people witnessed that a luminous sphere approached from East and descended to rest upon the tree by which Lucia, Franciso and Jacinta were praying. "*The sphere became a cloud from which shining petals fell once again, melting away to nothing before touching the outstretched hands of the multitude. The lady in the center of the sphere spoke with Lucia, promising a miracle on the thirteenth day of October. Then she ascended in her cocoon of light, and … sped straight up and disappeared into the sun. Among the thousands of witnesses were two priests who had come specifically to expose the now-famous miracles as a sham. The two devout skeptics were converted on the spot.*" *(Dan Millman & Childers, page 37)*

On October 13, an estimated seventy thousand people stood in the pouring rain in Cova da Iria waiting for the prophesied miracle. **At noon came a flash of light** and people close to the three children saw that their faces turned radiant, and that they conversed briefly with the lady in the sphere of light. Then the apparition ascended and the rain stopped. At this moment **thousands of people witnessed that the sun appeared as a shining silver disk that spun rapidly, throwing off brilliant beams of colored light in all directions.**

Fatima author William Thomas Walsh interviewed many eyewitnesses, and recounted the event as it was described to him:

"*While they gazed, the huge ball began to 'dance' … Now it whirled rapidly like a gigantic fire-wheel for some time with dizzy, sickening speed. Finally there appeared on the rim a border of crimson, which flung across the sky blood-red streamers of flame, reflecting to the earth, to the trees and shrubs, to the upturned faces and the clothes all sorts of brilliant colors in succession: green, red, orange, blue, violet, the whole spectrum. Madly gyrating in this manner three times, the fiery orb seemed to tremble, to shudder, and then to plunge precipitately, in a mighty zig-zag, toward the crowd.*" *(Dan Millman & Doug Childers, page 38)*

People got scared and flung themselves upon the muddy earth, praying for their lives. At the last moment, the silver disk reversed its descent and, at tremendous speed, ascended and flew into the sun. The event lasted about ten minutes. The astonished crowd was surprised to find their wet clothes suddenly completely dried. Besides, hundreds of people reported later, that they had been miraculously cured of various illnesses – cancers, wounds, and crippling diseases.

The miracle had been witnessed from as far away as thirty miles, where the lights of the "silver-disc sun" were clearly visible. People in other villages described objects and buildings reflecting the colors of the rainbow.

The Catholic Church started a formal investigation of the events of Fatima. Descriptions of the events were collected by Father John De Marchi, an Italian Catholic priest and researcher who spent seven years in Fátima, interviewing people. In *The Immaculate Heart,* published in 1952, De Marchi writes that, *'Reports do vary; impressions are in minor details confused, but none to our knowledge has directly denied the visible prodigy of the sun."* (https://en.wikipedia.org/wiki/Miracle_of_the_Sun)

De Marchi authored several books on the subject, reporting a great number of witness descriptions. A family member of Dr. Almeida Garrett, Professor of Natural Sciences, recounted that *"The sun's disc did not remain immobile. This was not the sparkling of a heavenly body, for it spun round on itself in a mad whirl when suddenly a clamor was heard from all the people. The sun, whirling, seemed to loosen itself from the firmament and sensation threateningly upon the earth as if to crush us with its huge fiery weight. The sensation during those moments was terrible."*

The event was declared of "supernatural character" by the Catholic Church in 1930 and Pope Pius XII approved the Fatima apparitions in 1940. Pope Pius XII claimed to have witnessed similar "Miracle of the Sun" on 30 October 1950, during a walk in the Vatican gardens. He saw the same miracle on 31 October, on 1 November and then again on 8 November. He confided this information to a number of Vatican cardinals and he even wrote about the apparitions in handwritten notes, discovered in 2008.

Skeptics who dismiss the events in Fatima as a miracle try to explain the phenomenon scientifically. For instance Benjamin Radford, a science writer asserts that psychological factors such as the power of suggestion can better explain the reported events and that the experience probably took place only in the minds of the people gathered in Cova da Iria. However, it is doubtful that thousands of people would be able to self-suggest the same paranormal experience at exact same time, during ten minutes.

August Meessen, professor of physics claims that the phenomena experienced in Fatima were optical effects caused by prolonged staring at the sun. But that day was cloudy with heavy rain, so the crowd had no chance to stare prolonged at the sun.

Reporters of principal newspapers were in Fatima/Cova da Iria when the phenomena occurred. *O Dia* reported: *"The sky had a certain greyish tint of pearl and a strange clearness filled the gloomy landscape, every moment getting gloomier. The sun seemed to be veiled with transparent gauze enabling us to look at it without difficult. The greyish tint ... began changing as if into a shining silver disc, that was growing slowly until it broke through the clouds. And the silvery sun, still shrouded in the same greyish lightness of gauze, was seen to rotate and wander."*

O Sècolo, a newspaper of Lisbon, also published a detailed recount of the events: *"From the height of the road where the people parked their carriages and where many hundreds stood, afraid to brave the muddy soil, we saw the immense multitude turn towards the sun at its highest, free of all clouds. The sun called to mind a plate of dull silver. It could be stared at without the least effort. It did not burn or blind ... the sun trembled and made some brusque unheard-of movements beyond all cosmic laws; the sun danced, is the typical expression of the peasants."* (John de Marchi, I.M.C., "The True Story of Fatima")

Some critics suggest that a combination of clouds, atmospheric sun-effects could have created the visual phenomena in Cova da Iria. Others stated that a cloud of dust from the Sahara caused the optical effects people could see. Those who said that perhaps it was an eclipse, did not take into consideration that the sun-phenomenon of Fatima has not been registered by any astronomical observatory either in Portugal or somewhere else on Earth.

Even if we suppose that it was a "local eclipse", one may wonder how could three children prophecy the exact datum of such an event? Besides no eclipse has ever cured people's illnesses and has neither had a great impact on thousands of people's lives as it happened in Fatima.

Another collective **experience of Madonna apparitions was recorded at St. Mark's Coptic Church in Zeitoun (Egypt)** beginning in 1968, ending in 1971. The first apparition occurred on the evening of April 2, 1968, when a Muslim bus mechanic named Farouk Mohammed Atwa, who worked across the street from St. Mark's Coptic Church, saw a woman on the top of the church. He and his workmate, who also saw the figure, thought that the woman was a nun contemplating suicide. Farouk ran to fetch the church pastor, while his workmate called the emergency squad. When they returned, the figure was gone; however, the rumour quickly spread that a luminous lady had appeared on the top of the church, so small crowds began to gather each night, waiting for her apparition.

On April 9, the woman, whom people believed to be the Madonna/Mary, reappeared, emanating an aura of light. The *"lady of light"* made hundreds of appearances over a period of two years, and finally disappeared in 1971. Hundreds of thousands witnessed the apparition and numerous photographic records exist. Church officials, and citizens of different faiths and social position, President Gamal Abdel Nassar, for instance, came to Zeitoun and witnessed a glowing female figure standing above the central dome of the church. The police performed investigations, but no device was found within a radius of fifteen miles capable of projecting the image, so there was no explanation for the phenomenon. The Egyptian government accepted the apparitions as true. Sociologists Robert Bartholomew and Erich Goode interpreted the apparitions as a case of mass hysteria: *"It appears that the Maria observers were predisposed by religious background and social expectation to interpreting the light displays as related to the Virgin Mary." (www.skeptically.org/skepticism/id11.html)* But how can a Muslim, a Jew or an atheist observer be predisposed by religious background and social expectation to see a Madonna apparition on the top of a Catholic Church?

Bishop Samuel, official investigator for the Coptic Christian Church, witnessed the apparition numerous times and was deeply moved by his experiences. He wrote: *"The scene was overwhelming and magnificent. The apparition walked toward the west, sometimes moving its hands and blessing and sometimes bowing repeatedly. A halo of light surrounded its head. I saw some glittering beings around the apparition. They looked like stars."* (Dan Millman & Doug Childers, Bridge Between Worlds, page 109)

Bishop Athanasius, sent by the Coptic Pope Kryllos VI to investigate, reported: *"There she was, five or six meters above the dome, high in the sky, full figure, like a phosphorous statue, but not so stiff as a statue. There was movement of the body and of the clothing ... One would estimate the crowd at 100,000 ... Our Lady looked to the north; she waved her hand; she blessed the people, sometimes in the direction where we stood. Her garments swayed in the wind. ... It was something really supernatural, very, very heavenly."* (Bridge Between Worlds, page 109)

Skeptics doubt individual or collective supernatural experiences connected to a Madonna apparition or other kind of unexplainable event. They do not think that "light miracles" also occur in the subatomic particle accelerators in Switzerland, or on television screens when "light particles" sent from media studios in America cross oceans and mountains and then appear as "visible figures" of people who move and talk. If man is able to make such a "miracle", why should God not be able to send a Madonna figure to our planet?

Dr. Jacques Vallée, French astrophysicist, who had worked in an observatory outside Paris, had studied records of different extraordinary phenomena from various cultures and historical eras. He concluded that, from earliest times to the present, humanity has been visited by apparently intelligent entities that have appeared in various guises, yet whose nature and origins remain a mystery.

The story of **the apparitions in Lourdes** is connected to *Bernadette Soubirous* who in 1858 reported a vision of the so called Our Lady of Lourdes. Bernadette was a simple 14-years-old peasant girl, who, when collecting some firewood near the Grotto of Massabielle/Lourdes, had an **apparition of a "lady in light"**, whom she described as a "small maiden" in white, with a golden rosary and blue belt and two golden roses at her feet. In subsequent visitations the Lady asked her to do different things.

She asked Bernadette to dig in the ground and drink from the spring she found there. Although the water was muddy at first, it became increasingly clean, and soon the word spread about the "miraculous water" with healing effect in Lourdes. The water was given to medical patients of all kinds and many reports of certified miraculous cures followed.

Dr. Alexis Carrel, a scientist and later a Nobel Prize winner, did not believe that organic diseases such as cancer or tuberculosis could be cured by "miraculous water" and by faith alone. In 1903, he traveled to Lourdes in order to investigate the phenomenon directly, examining patients before and after they went to the "holy grotto". Marie Ferrand, an unfortunate girl in the final stages of tuberculosis would be his first test case. *"I know her history – her whole family died of the same disease,"* Dr. Carrel said to a young medic and past classmate he met in Lourdes. *"She has tubercular sores, lesions of the lungs, and now has a peritonitis diagnosed … Her condition is very grave … She may die any moment. If such a case were cured, it would indeed be a miracle."*

In his book *Man: The Unknown* – based on detailed notes he took as the events occurred – Dr. Carrel described what happened when they took Marie Ferrand to the holy grotto. *"The ministering priest was kneeling down, facing the line of patients and the crowds beyond. He lifted his arms and held them out like a cross. He was young; … 'Holy Virgin, heal our sick!' he cried out … the crowd responded with a cry … Here and there, people held out their arms … The atmosphere* was tense with expectancy ... A wind seemed to blow through the crowd; intangible, silent, powerful, irresistible, it swept over the people."

Dr. Carrel feared to immerse his patient, Marie Ferrand in the grotto, so he and the stretcher bearer instead poured water from the grotto over her head. Then he observed his patient intently and with the objectivity of a physician. Later he wrote: *"There was no longer any doubt. Marie Ferrand's condition was improving so much that she was scarcely recognizable ... In a few minutes she raised her head, looked around, moved her limbs a little, then turned over on her side, without having shown the least sign of pain ... A dying girl is recovering"*

Dr. Carrel, together with two other doctors examined the patient thoroughly when she returned to the hospital and concluded that, except for the weakness generated by her prolonged illness, she seemed completely normal. **She was cured.**

This miraculous healing caused a spiritual dilemma and a crisis in Dr. Carrel's soul. If he reported what he had experienced in Lourdes, he risked the loss of prestige and respect among his colleagues. Yet, if he withheld the truth, he risked losing his integrity and self-respect.

The miraculous healing of Marie Ferrand in Lourdes was a turning point in the life and career of Dr. Carrel, who later wrote: *"We must liberate man from the cosmos created by the genius of physicists, astronomers, that cosmos in which, since the Renaissance, he has been imprisoned. We know that we ... extend outside the physical continuum ... In time, as in space, the individual stretches out beyond the frontiers of his body ... He also belongs to another world."* (Dan Millman & Doug Childers: Bridge Between Worlds, page184)

The ancients were more humble as people in our time are, when searching the mysteries of the universe. They knew that it is almost impossible to find out the whole truth about the invisible world that in religious context is called The Realm of God. According to *Paul the Apostle*, **"now we see in a mirror, dimly**, *but then face to face. Now I know in part, but then I shall know just as I also am known. And now abide faith, hope, love, these three; but the greatest of these is love." (1 Corinthians 13:12–13)*

THE MULTITUDE OF GODS

Galilee, where Jesus grew up, was a multicultural and a pluralistic society where several cultures and religions mixed. There was only 6 km distance from Nazareth to Sephoris which was at the time of Jesus a large, Roman influenced city. Reza Aslan (born 1972), an Iranian-American author, religious studies scholar, describes Sephoris at the time of Jesus, as a rich and cosmopolitan place, deeply influenced by Greek culture and "surrounded by a panoply of races and religions." The site holds a rich and diverse historical and architectural legacy that includes Hellenistic, Jewish, Roman, Byzantine and other cultures' influences. In late Antiquity, it was believed to be the birthplace of Mary, mother of Jesus.

According to unauthorized scripts, Jesus was very intelligent and sometimes he knew more than the teachers of the school he attended. Maybe it was his thirst for more knowledge that made him leave the parental home when he was twelve years old and travel to the Far East.

There are documents reporting that Jesus, when he was twelve or thirteen, left for India and Tibet, maybe in the company of Joseph of Arimathea, a rich man who was a friend of Joseph. According to some scripts, Jesus stayed abroad for about seventeen years.

During his long journeys through Persia and Asia he had opportunity to come into contact with and learn about foreign cultures and religions, as Hinduism, Buddhism, Taoism and Confucianism.

It is documented that, after studying the Vedas and the cults of the Brahma priests, he criticized them for worshiping so many gods. Three researchers, Nicolas Notovitch (1858-after 1916), Swami Abhedananda (1866–1939) and Nicholas Roerich, journeyed to India and Tibet and visited the Himis monastery, where Buddhist monks showed them very old scripts about Jesus' staying in India.

According to these scripts Jesus/Issa said *"that man had filled the temples with abominations. In order to pay homage to metals and stones* (that is statues), *man sacrificed fellows in whom dwells a spark of the Supreme Spirit." (Nicholas Roerich)*

"... the white priests of Brahma made Jesus a Joyous welcome and they taught him to read and understand the Vedas", but when they wanted him to worship their gods, he preached against the Brahmans and said, *"Worship not the idols"* , *" ... the Eternal Spirit, comprehends the one and indivisible soul of the universe, which alone creates, contains, and vivifies all." (Nicolai Notovitch: "The Unknown Life of Saint Issa/Jesus" – Script at Himis convent)*

The Brahma priests respected him, but they feared that his teaching might have a great impact on people, and therefore some of them planned to kill him, but *"Issa, forewarned, departed from this place by night. Afterwards, Issa went to Nepal and into the Himalayan mountains ..."(Nicholas Roerich)*

Jesus' mission both in the Far East and later in Judea was **to defend monotheism by combating polytheism,** as he knew that the worshiping of many gods and their attributes was prevalent in his time.

He surely knew for instance about Zeus, the Greek God, Jupiter, Minerva and other gods of the Romans, as well as about the multitude of gods adored in Egypt.

Zeus, Greek God of the Sky and King of Gods is often referred as the "Father of Gods and men. He is a king of Mount Olympus, where he rules the world and imposes his will onto gods and mortals. He controls lightning and thunder, similar to Israel's God, Jahwe.

Zeus mated with many goddesses and mortals. He was regarded as wise, fair, just and merciful, but he was also easily angered and could be very destructive.

It is remarkable that the word for God in Rumanian, *Dumnezeu*, includes the name of Zeus. *Dumne* originates from Latin *domine*, so, surprisingly and unfortunately the Romanian Orthodox Christians worship "Lord Zeus"; they also use the term Domnul (from Latin *Domine)* for Lord.

Volumes of Jewish and Christian academic writings have accumulated describing **the God of Israel** according to the Bible. However, after the 1920s, when a series of clay tablets were found in the Tell of Ugarit (modern Ras Shamra on the Mediterranean coast of northern Syria) academics and theologians had to change many of their old opinions and had to reinterpret their concept and belief of Israel's God. First of all they had to revise the attributes of the different "gods" with the different names in the Old Testament.

Rabbinic Judaism describes seven names which are very holy: – the JHWH, read Jehovah/Jahwe or Adonai, – El (God), Eloah (God), Elohim (gods), Shaddai (God Almighty) Ehyeh, and Tzevaot – Sebaoth (God of Hosts). There are other names too, but they are considered mere epithets or titles reflecting different aspects of God.

The name of God used most often in the Hebrew Bible is JHWH, read as Jehovah or Yahweh. According to Jewish tradition, JHWH is often named as Adonai (Lord) out of respect and even Christian theologians and translators of the Bible often use the term "Lord" for JHWH.

Similar to Zeus, **Yahweh** controls lighting and thunder when revealing itself:

"Then it came to pass on the third day, in the morning, that there were thunderings and lightnings, and a thick cloud on the mountain;

and the sound of trumpet was very loud, so that all the people who were in the camp trembled.

And Moses brought the people out of the camp to meet with God, and they stood at the foot of the mountain.

Now Mount Sinai was completely in smoke, because the Lord descended upon it in fire. Its smoke ascended like the smoke of a furnace, and the whole mountain quaked greatly.

And when the blast of the trumpet sounded long and became louder and louder, Moses spoke, and God answered him by voice"(Exodus 19:16–19)

For the Canaanites and the ancient Levantine region as a whole, **El or Il** was the supreme god, the father of mankind and all creatures. Similarly to Zeus, he also fathers many gods, is the husband of Asheram and has many other wives. El has many children, but his major son is Hadad. Their **symbol** is **the bull.**

In the Ugaritic Ba'al cycle **El** is introduced **dwelling in a tent (not a temple!)** on Mount Lel. According to another text, El builds a desert sanctuary with his children and his two wives, suggesting that at one point **El was a desert god.**

The fragmentary text R.S. 24.258 describes a banquet to which El invites other gods and then disgraces himself by becoming outrageously drunk. Two other gods, Thukamuna and Shanuma help him to get home.

El is a kind and happy god, but he becomes weak when getting older. This might be the explanation why **Moses does not want the people of Israel to worship El,** the golden calf god fashioned while he was on the Mountain of Sinai.

"Now when the people saw that Moses delayed coming down from the mountain, the people gathered together to Aaron, and said to him, 'Come make us gods that shall go before us; for as for this Moses, the man who brought us up out of the land of Egypt, we do not know what has become of him.'

And Aaron said to them, 'Break off the golden ear rings which are in the ears of your wives, your sons, and your daughters, and bring them to me.' …

*And he received the gold from their hand, and **he fashioned it** ... and **made a molded calf. Then they said, 'This is your god, O Israel, that brought you out of the land of** Egypt'*
So when Aaron saw it, he built and altar before it." (Exodus 32:1 ... 5)

When Moses comes back and sees what Aaron and the people have done, he gets very angry:

"So Moses' anger became hot, and he cast the tablets out of his hands and broke them at the foot of the mountain. Then he took the calf which they have made, burned it in the fire, and ground it to powder ..." (Exodus 32:19)

Moses destroys the golden calf, the symbol of El. He needs to act in the name of a powerful LORD God of Israel:

*"And he said to them, 'Thus says the LORD God of Israel: ' Let every man put his sword on his side, and go in and out from entrance to entrance throughout the camp, and **let every man kill his brother, every man his companion, and every man his neighbour.'***

*So the sons of Levi did according to the word of Moses. And **about three thousand men of the people fell that day.***

Then Moses said, 'Consecrate yourselves today to the LORD, that he may bestow on you a blessing this day, for every man has opposed his son and his brother.'" (Exodus 32:27-29)

There are several stories in the Old Testament recounting Moses', his son Joshua's and other **religious leaders' cruelty legitimized by the LORD Sabaoth.**

Theologians maintain that all the names and titles referring to the God of Israel reveal an aspect of Jehovah's nature and attributes and so does **Jahwe Sabaoth** who actually is the commander of vast forces. He is the **Lord of the armies.** Ecclesiastics assert that the correct interpretation is that Sabaoth is the Lord of the heavenly armies, but reading about all the cruel genocides carried out in the name of LORD Sebaoth, we doubt the clergy's statement. We do not think on peace in heaven, but on all the war calamities and sufferings on Earth when in the name of this god people fight against each other, may it be Jews, Muslims or Christians.

The attributes of the LORD of Israel is worded in the remarkable song Moses sings on his death-bed, expressing a fearful god-image. We read:

"Now see that I, even I, am he,
And there is no God besides me;
I kill and I make alive;
I wound and I heal;

I will make arrows drunk with blood,
And my sword shall devour flesh,
With the blood of the slain and the captives,
From the heads of the leaders of the enemy." (Deuteronomy 32:39 ... 42)

Moses sings of a bloodthirsty god of war, whose worship was important in the struggle for the Promised Land. Unfortunately, this god-image has been handed down to several leaders of different religions, as well as to the "leaders of the world".

Joshua, the successor of Moses acts and talks in a very similar way to his predecessor when he occupies Jericho. He says according to a text in the Book of Joshua:

"Shout, for the LORD has given you the city!

Now the city shall be doomed by the LORD to destruction, it and all who are in it. ...

And they utterly destroyed all that was in the city, both man and woman, young and old, ox and sheep and donkey, with the edge of the sword ... they burned the city and all that was in it with fire. Only the silver and gold, and the vessels of bronze and iron, they put into the treasury of the house of the LORD:" (Joshua 6:16 ... 24)

Clergymen often use the story of Jericho as an example of the wonderful acts of the LORD towards all those whom he loves and those who trust in him, but not a word is mentioned about the victims, men, women and children who had to pay with their lives. In the Preface of the Book of Joshua (Swedish Bible, translated and edited in 2000), we can read:

"Like all historical accounts in the Old Testament, the content (of the Book of Joshua) *is a combination of reporting historical events and blessings. Therefore, the perspective is theological.*"

One wonders which blessing and what theological perspective the author of the Preface has in mind when she/he reads the following texts in *Joshua:*

"On that day **Joshua took Makkedah,** *and struck it and its king with the edge of the sword. He utterly destroyed them – all the people who were in it. He let none remain …*

So Joshua conquered all the land: … he left none remaining, but utterly **destroyed all that breathed, as the LORD God of Israel had commanded.**" *(Joshua 10:28 … 40)*

"As the LORD had commanded Moses his servant, so Moses commanded Joshua, and so Joshua did. He left nothing undone of all that the LORD had commanded Moses." (Joshua 11:15)

The LORD of the hosts, Sabaoth admonishes Saul, the first king of Israel, who had defeated the Ammonites, but did not carry out *herem* – that is total annihilation of the enemy, to kill men and women, infants and nursing children. We read in the 1 Samuel book:

"**Thus says the LORD of hosts**:
Now go and attack Amalek, and utterly destroy all that they have, and **do not spare them. But kill both man and woman, infant and nursing child, ox and sheep, camel and donkey.**" *(1 Samuel 15:2 … 3)*

It is doubtful whether Israel was all that successful in its warfare as the Bible authors describe. It is more likely that the land of Canaan was occupied only partly and by degrees. At any rate, violence, destruction and genocide should not be regarded as a fulfillment of the commandments of God, especially not according to what Jesus teaches about **THE ONE WHO IS LIGHT, PEACE AND LOVE.**

The fierceness of the God of Israel contrasts with **Jesus' no violence attitude** that is evident in the texts reporting his arrest in the garden of Gethsemane. When a great multitude comes with swords and clubs from the chief priests in order to arrest Jesus, one of his disciples (maybe Peter), *"drew his sword, struck the servant of the high priest, and cut off his ear.*

Then Jesus said to him, **'Put your sword in its place, for all who take the sword will perish by the sword.'"** (Matthew 26:50 ... 52)

The best evidence of Jesus' rejecting the wars and genocides carried through in the name of the LORD of the hosts, is a text reporting his arguing with the Scribes and Pharisees. Once, when he almost convinced a few of them to believe him and to be his disciples, their conversation took suddenly a hostile turn:

"Then Jesus said to those Jews who believed him, 'If you abide in my word, you are my disciples indeed. And you shall know the truth, and the truth shall make you free.'

They answered him, 'We are Abraham's descendants, and have never been in bondage to anyone. How can you say, 'You will be made free?'

Jesus answered them, 'Most assuredly, I say to you, whoever commits sin is a slave of sin.

'I know that you are Abraham's descendants, but you seek to kill me, because my word has no place in you.

'I speak what I have seen with **my Father,** *and you do what you have seen with* **your father.***'*

They answered and said to him, 'Abraham is our father.' Jesus said to them, 'If you were Abraham's children, you would do the works of Abraham. But now you seek to kill me, a man who has told you the truth which I heard from God. Abraham did not do this.

You do the deeds of your father'.

Then **they said to him,** *'We are not born of fornication;* **we have one Father – God.'**

Jesus said to them, 'If God were your Father, you would love me, for I proceeded forth and came from God.'

*You are of **your father the devil,** and the desires of your father you want to do.* **He was a murderer from the beginning,** *and does not stand in the truth, because there is no truth in him. When he speaks a lie, he speaks from his own resources, for he is a liar and the father of it ..."* (John 8:31 ... 44)

Jesus' challenging words upset the Jews who then *"took up stones to throw at him: but Jesus hid himself and went out of the temple ..."*

Jesus often argued with the Pharisees and the scribes presenting his contradictory opinion concerning the Jew's religion and the religious leaders' hypocritical attitudes. Once he said to them:

"Woe to you, scribes and Pharisees, hypocrites! For you cleanse the outside of the cup and dish, but inside they are full of extortion and self-indulgence ...

Woe to you, scribes and Pharisees, hypocrites! For you are like white-washed tombs which indeed appear beautiful outwardly, but inside are full of dead men's bones and all uncleanness.

Even so you also outwardly appear righteous to men, but inside you are full of hypocrisy and lawlessness." (Matthew 23:25 ... 28)

If Jesus had been a true, faithful Rabbi, as Christian theologians assert, then he had never dared to call the scribes and Pharisees hypocrites and he would have not said that their father was the devil and a murderer, probably making allusion to all the genocides reported in the Old Testament. His sharp disputes with the religious leaders have surely been one of the main reasons that the chief-priests and the Sanhedrin took the decision to get rid of him. They also feared that Jesus' new doctrines would turn the Jews from the traditions of the ancestors. They chose the cruelest and most shameful execution form, the crucifixion as their purpose was not only to kill Jesus but also to humiliate him.

"WHO DO THE CROWDS SAY THAT I AM?" (Luke 9:18)

When Jesus was curious about what people thought of him, he asked the disciples, *"Who do the crowds say that I am?"* The disciples answered that people thought he was John the Baptist or one of the old prophets who has risen again: *"And it happened, as he was alone praying, that his disciples joined him, and he asked them, saying,* **'Who do the crowds say that I am?'** *So they answered and said, 'John the Baptist, but some say Elijah; and others say that one of the old prophets has risen again.'"* (Luke 9:18–19)

As the disciples do not mention that the crowds thought Jesus was the Messiah, we may conclude that the Jews did not think of him to be the Immanuel the prophets of The Old Testament had talked about. The answer of the disciples also make evident that the crowd mixed up Jesus with John the Baptist who was a well-known hermit prophet baptizing people in Jordan. The disciples' assertion that the crowd thought Jesus was a reincarnated prophet, suggests that the Jews believed in reincarnation.

Jesus also wanted to know what the disciples thought of him, so he asked them: **"But who do you say that I am?"**

There are different versions of the disciples' supposed answer on the question. In *The Gospel of Thomas* we read*:* "Simon Peter said to him: 'You are like **a just messenger.'** Matthew said to him, 'You are like **a wise philosopher.'** Thomas said to him, '**Teacher (rabbi)**, my mouth is utterly unable to say what you are like.' Jesus said, '**I am not your teacher** … And he took him, and withdrew, and spoke three sayings to him. When Thomas came back to his friends, they asked him, 'What did Jesus say to you?' Thomas said to them, 'If I tell you one of the sayings he spoke to me, you will pick up rocks and stone me, ..." (The Gospel of Thomas, NH scriptures, page 141)

Jesus rejects being called a teacher/rabbi as that was the title of the Pharisees and scholars educated in *halakhah (Jewish law)*. A rabbi instructed the Jewish community in *halakhah*, answered questions and resolved disputes regarding the Jewish laws that had been generally agreed upon by Jewish scholars over the centuries. **Jesus preferred to be called *Master*.** An Ascended Master was believed to be a spiritually enlightened being that has incarnated as ordinary human. A Master does not teach halakhah (Jewish law) but delivers knowledge about spirituality.

According to *Luke,* Peter declared Jesus to be the Messiah, but the Master *"strictly warned and commanded them to tell this to no one."* (Luke 9:20.21) There are more texts confirming that Jesus did not want the disciples to use the term "Messiah" referring to him. In the Gospel of Mark nothing is mentioned about Jesus' warning. We only read that the Master *"began to teach them that the Son of Man must suffer many things, and be rejected by the elders and chief priests and scribes, and be killed, and after three days rise again. He spoke this word openly. And Peter took him aside and began to rebuke him. But when he had turned around and looked at his disciple, he rebuked Peter saying, 'Get behind me, Satan! For you are not mindful of the things of God, but the things of men.'"* (Mark: 8:31 ... 33)

It is not only Mark who recounts that Jesus warned about the peril he will be exposed to. According to *The First Revelation of James*, two days before the crucifixion Jesus met his stepbrother, James and said to him: *"'They will arrest me the day after tomorrow, but my deliverance will be near.' James said, ' ... you said, *They will arrest me. What can I do? 'He said ..., 'Don't be afraid, James. You too will be arrested.* **Leave Jerusalem, for this city always gives the cup of bitterness to the children of light. This is the dwelling place of many archons ..."** (NH, The First Revelation of James, 25,9 ..., page 324) James did not listen to the Master's caution; he stayed in Jerusalem and he too was executed by the priests.

In *The Gospel of Matthew* we read a totally different recount concerning Jesus' reaction on Peter's asserting that the Master was the Messiah. In this gospel we read that Jesus praised Peter for his statement: *"Blessed are you, Simon Bar-Jonah, for flesh and blood has not revealed this to you, but my Father who is in heaven. And I also say to you that you are Peter, and on this rock I will build my church, and the gates of Hades shall not prevail against it. And I will give you the keys of the kingdom of heaven … Then he commanded his disciples that they should tell no one that he was Jesus the Christ"* (Matthew 16:15 … 20)

It is unlikely that Jesus blessed Peter for his statement and promised him to be "the rock" of his church because, according to *The Gospel of Mark*, the Master avoided any hierarchical differentiation of the disciples. We read:

"Then James and John, the sons of Zebedee, came to him, saying: 'Teacher, we want you to do for us whatever we ask.' And he said to them, 'What do you want me to do for you?' They said to him, 'Grant us that we may sit, one on your right hand and the other on your left, in your glory.' But Jesus said to them, 'You do not know what you ask … to sit on my right hand and on my left is not mine to give, but it is for those for whom it is prepared.' And when the ten heard it, they began to be greatly displeased with James and John. But Jesus called them to himself and said to them,' You know that those who are considered rulers over the Gentiles lord it over them, and their great ones exercise authority over them. Yet it shall not be so among you; but whoever desires to become great among you shall be your servant. And whoever of you desires to be first shall be slave of all.'" (Mark 10:35 … 44)

The appointment of Peter as the rock on which the Church is to be built, has probably not been the idea of Matthew, the evangelist. The original text might have been revised and completed later when the institutional Catholic Church wanted to exalt the pope as direct successor of Peter and by that of Jesus Christ. The explanation of the contradictory accounts of the same story may be that the gospel authors and later editors had different backgrounds, information sources and purposes. The complicated hierarchy systems in the different Christian denominations show that the words of the Master have not gained hearing. For 2000 years popes, cardinals, patriarchs, bishops and many other dignitaries of the Church have ruled as the Gentiles, exercising authority over each other and over the Christians all over the world. They have lived and ruled after worldly habits and have failed to establish real spiritual communities as Jesus had wished it.

There are texts suggesting that at the beginning the chief priests, scribes and the Pharisees did not know who Jesus actually was and what his background was when he came to Jerusalem and started teaching people and doing miracles. We read about their uncertainty in the *Gospel of John*: *"Now the Jew's Feast of Tabernacles was at hand.* **His brothers therefore said to him, 'Depart from here and go into Judea**, *that your disciples also may see the works that you are doing. 'For no one does anything in secret while he himself seeks to be known openly. If you do these things, show yourself to the world.'* **For even his brothers did not believe in him**. *Then Jesus said to them, 'My time has not yet come, but your time is always ready. The world cannot hate you, but it hates me because I testify of it that its works are evil. You go up to this feast. I am not yet going up to this feast, for my time has not yet fully come.' When he had said these things to them, he remained in Galilee. But when his brothers had gone up, then he also went up to the feast, not openly, but as it were in secret. Then the Jews sought him at the feast, and said, 'Where is he?'* **And there was much murmuring among the people concerning him. Some said, 'He is good'; others said, 'No, on the contrary, he deceives the people.'**

However, no one spoke openly of him for fear of the Jews. Now about the middle of the feast **Jesus went up into the temple and taught**. *And* **the Jews marveled, saying, 'How does this man know letters, never having studied?'** *Jesus answered them and said, 'My doctrine is not mine, but his who sent me' … And* **many of the people believed in him**, *and said, 'When the Christ comes, will he do more signs than these which this man has done?' The Pharisees heard the crowd murmuring these things concerning him, and the Pharisees and the chief priests sent officers to take him … Then the officers came to the chief priests and Pharisees, who said to them, 'Why have you not brought* *him?' The officers answered, '**No man ever spoke like this man!**' Then the Pharisees answered them, 'Are you also deceived? Have any of the rulers or the Pharisees believed in him? But this crowd that does not know the law, is accursed. 'Nicodemus ... said to them, 'Does our law judge a man before it hears him and knows what he is doing?' They answered and said to him, 'Are you also from Galilee? Search and look, for no prophet has arisen out of Galilee.' (John 7:1 ... 52)*

According to this text, the Pharisees and the chief priest do not mention anything about Jesus belonging to king David's family, neither of his being born in Bethlehem in Judea. They insist on his coming from Galilee which they considered to be a place from where no prophet has arisen. It is noteworthy that the chief priests as well as the Jewish Council (Sanhedrin) had control of the genealogical tablets of the Jews, so they surely had checked and tried to find out Jesus' family background especially when people came up with the rumor that he would be the Messiah. They were certainly confused when the officers reported that "No man ever spoke like this man!" as they considered Jesus to be a deceiver whose doctrines threatened the Jewish religious traditions.

Who was this Jesus who had such an impact on the crowds and troubled the Jewish religious leaders? What do we know about his family background and genealogy?

It is not easy to answer these questions as, in spite of the abundance of scripts about Jesus, there are very few reliable sources reporting about his family background. It is easier to get information about the spiritual Jesus coming from another sphere as the Son of Light, than the man Jesus.

The New Testament supplies very little information about the background of **Mary, Jesus' mother**. It is supposed that she came from Cana of Galilee, where she had relatives and where Jesus followed her to a wedding, (John 2).

The Apocrypha *The Proto-Gospel of James* tells the story of **Mary, the child** who is taken to the temple in order to learn weaving ritual clothes for the priests. This task was mostly performed by virgins who had no monthly bleeding. According to

Jewish tradition, a woman, who entered the temple of the Lord when having monthly bleeding, polluted the temple. Mary, who was praying and blessing God without intermission while working with the wool-work, stayed there until she was twelve years old when the council of priests said: *"'Behold Mary is become twelve years old in the temple of the Lord. What then shall we do with her? Lest she pollute the sanctuary of the Lord.'"*

According to the Apocrypha, the temple priests arranged the marriage of Mary and **Joseph** who at the beginning refused to take such a young girl in his home. He said: *"I have sons, and I am an old man, but she is a girl: lest I became a laughing-stock to the children of Israel." (Jesus, The Unauthorized Version: The Proto-Gospel of James, page 40)*

The priests insist by quoting threatening texts from the Old Testament, so Joseph finally *"took her to keep her for himself. And Joseph said unto Mary: 'Lo, I have received thee out of the temple of the Lord: and now do I leave thee in my house, and I go away to build my buildings and I will come again unto thee. The Lord shall watch over thee." (The Proto-Gospel of James, page 40)*

According to another Apocrypha, *The History of Joseph the Carpenter*, Joseph had four sons and two daughters. *"Now these are the names – Judas, Justus, James, and Simon. The names of the two daughters were Assia and Lydia. At length the wife of righteous Joseph, a woman intent on the divine glory in all her works, departed this life."* (page 41) *"Now Justus and Simon, the elder sons of Joseph, were married, and had families of their own. Both daughters were likewise married, and lived in their own houses. So there remained in Joseph's house, Judas and James the Less ..." (page 42 ... 43)*

When Mary came to Joseph's house, she *"found James the Less ... sad on account of the loss of his mother, and she brought him up. Hence Mary was called the mother of James" (Jesus – The Unauthorised Version: Jesus's Parents, page 42)*

Maybe Joseph's wife had died when giving birth to her youngest child, and James was probably one or two years old when Mary came to their home. According to *The Second Revelation of James*, Mary said to Jesus, that he and James *"were both nourished with the same milk"*, which means that Mary suckled not only the baby Jesus, but James too. James self-recounted about this according to *The Second Revelation of James:* "*One time when I was sitting and meditating, the one whom you hated and persecuted opened the door and came in to me, and he said to me, 'Hello, my brother; brother, hello.' As I raised my head to look at him, mother said to me, 'Don't be afraid, my son, because he said to you, 'My brother'. You were both nourished with the same milk. That is why he says to me, 'My mother.' He is not a stranger to us; he is your stepbrother.*" (NH, The Second Revelation of James, page 335–336)

The explanation of James not recognizing his stepbrother may be that Jesus had been away in Asia during seventeen years. At the end of the 1800 century, researchers found very old documents preserved in a Buddhist convent in Tibet which reports about Jesus leaving Galilee when he was 12, as mentioned earlier, and his staying in India and Tibet until he was about 29 years old. Both James and Jesus were adults when they met again, so it is understandable why they did not recognize each other when Jesus suddenly appeared.

There are only guesses concerning **Jesus' biological father** as there are **no sure facts** accepted by all historians and theologians. To avoid the various speculations, the theological explanation is that Jesus was conceived of the Holy Spirit. This doctrine need not to be completely wrong as no living being can exist without "the breath of life", i.e. the life giving spirit. Those who laugh at Mary's virginity should think that Mary certainly was a virgin when she got pregnant at age 12 or 13.

There are Jewish scriptures – *the Talmud, the Mishna and the Gemara* containing speculations about Jesus' parents, but researchers have questioned the reliability of the information delivered in these scripts. The Talmud, for instance, was written several centuries later, between the years 170–600, so the information about Jesus' parents is probably based on gossips and not historical facts. We also know that the stories of Talmud were edited during a time when there were sharp contradictions between Christianity and Judaism. Spiteful and sarcastic disputations and discrediting assertions about Jesus' descent and his person were not unusual at that time.

In the 2nd century, *Celsus*, a Greek philosopher, wrote that Jesus' father was a Roman soldier named Panthera. His wide ranging criticism of Christianity, for instance the assertion that the teachings of Jesus included nothing new and that they were repetitions of sayings of the Greek philosophers, gives evidence of Celsus'negative opinion of the Master. Celsus' work was lost, but the story is mentioned in Origen's work, *Contra Celsum* (Against Celsus).

The book *Toledot Yeshu*, edited in the Middle Ages, was *an anti-Christian satirical chronicle of Jesus;* the author accuses Jesus of illegitimate birth and says that he was the son of Pandera or Pantera.

According to the *Jerusalem Talmud*, Rabbi Hisda and the Wise were confused when discussing Jesus' family name as they did not know if he was *"Ben Stada"* which means "the son of Stada" or he was *"Ben Pantera"* – "the son of Pantera".They also have disgracing comments about Miriam, i.e. Mary. *"... Ben Stada is Ben Pantera. Rabbi Hisda said, 'The husband was Stada, the lover was Pantera.' The husband was 'actually' Pappos ben Judah, the mother was Stada. The mother was Miriam "Mary" the dresser of women's hair. As we say in Pumbeditha, 'She has been false to satath da, her husband." (b. Shabbat 104b) (source of the quotation: (https://en.wikipedia.org/wiki/Tiberius_Julius_Abdes_Pantera)*

In 1238 *Nicholas Donin*, an intelligent young Jewish man who was critical to the religious traditions and scripts of his ancestors, was excommunicated from the ghetto of Paris by Rabbi Yechiel in 1225. Having lived for ten years in excommunication, though still clinging to Judaism, he finally converted to Christianity and later joined the Franciscan Order. In 1238 Donin journeyed to Rome, met Pope Gregory IX, and denounced the Talmud. He stated his charges in thirty-five articles in which he denounced the virulent attacks in Talmud on Mary, on Jesus' family background and the divinity of Jesus.

After about one year of examination of the validity of Donin's charges, Pope Gregory IX and King Louis IX ordered a public debate where four of the most distinguished rabbis of France had to answer Donin. The result of the debate was that the commission condemned the Talmud to be burned.

The curiosity of the researchers about Tiberius Julius Abdes Pantera as the biological father of Jesus arouse again after one day in October 1859, when during the construction of a railroad in Bingerbrück in Germany, the tombstones of nine Roman soldiers were accidentally discovered. The most exciting tombstone was the one which had the inscription of a soldier named Tiberius Julius Abdes Pantera:

Tib(berius) Jul(ius) Abdes Pantera Sidonia ann(orum) LXII stipen(diorum) XXXX miles exs(ignifer?) coh(orte) I sagittariorum h(ic) s(itus) e(st>)

The researchers made detailed analysis and interpretations of every word of the inscription. According to the inscription, Pantera was from Sidonia, which is identified with Sidon in Phoenicia. He probably joined the first cohort of archers in Judea at the time when Roman army enlistments were for 25 years, however Pantera on the tombstone served 40 years in the army until his death at 62. As the Cohort I Sagittariorum was first stationed in Judaea until year 9, some researchers conclude that the person named on the tombstone could have been the biological father of Jesus.

Historians and ecclesiastics of the Catholic Church reject the assumption that Jesus' biological father was a Roman soldier. However, this theory could be a plausible answer to the question **why Pilate was so reluctant in condemning Jesus to crucifixion.** As Romans were not allowed to be crucified, Pilate must have been very confused when hearing that Jesus' mother was Aramaic and his father was probably Roman.

Pilate's reluctance is evident when he is confronted with the Jews' crying out "Crucify him!"

We read in John 19:

"… 'Behold the man!' Therefore, when the chief priests and officers saw him, they cried out, saying, 'Crucify him, crucify him!' Pilate said to them, 'You take him and crucify him, for I find no fault in him.' The

Jews answered him, 'We have a law, and according to our law he ought to die, because he made himself the Son of God.' Therefore, when Pilate heard that saying, he was more afraid ..." (John 19:1-8)

As the term "Son of God", in Latin Divi Filius, indicated the divine son-ship of a person, Pilate did not know what to think of Jesus who was worshiped by the crowd as a divine person and accused by the chief priests for being a deceiver.

According to *The Gospel of Luke,* when Pilate heard that Jesus was from Galilee, he immediately tried to escape judging him; *"he knew that he belonged to Herod's jurisdiction",* so *"he sent him to Herod, who was also in Jerusalem at that time.*

Now when Herod saw Jesus, he was exceedingly glad; for he had desired for a long time to see him, because he had heard many things about him, and he hoped to see some miracle done by him. Then he questioned him with many words, but he answered him nothing. Then **Herod,** *with his men of war, treated him with contempt and mocked him, arrayed him in a gorgeous robe, and* **sent him back to Pilate.**" *(Luke 23:7 ... 11)*

Pilate called together the chief priests and other leaders of the Sanhedrin and declared once more, *"'indeed, having examined him in your presence, I have found no fault in this man concerning those things of which you accused him; no, neither did Herod, for I sent you back to him; and indeed nothing worthy of death has been done by him. I will therefore chastise him and release him' ... And they all cried out at once, saying, 'Away with this man, and release to us Barabbas' – Pilate, therefore, wishing to release Jesus, again called out to them.*

But they shouted, saying, 'Crucify him, crucify him!'" (Luke 23:13 ... 21)

Pilate's task was to punish troublemakers and agitators in the Roman Empire. If Jesus had indeed acted as the long-awaited king of Israel from the House of David, the Jews would have praised and accepted him as their Messiah and he would have awakened Pilate's suspicions. But all this did not happen, Pilate did not suspect Jesus being a troublemaker.

The executors were Roman soldiers, but it was the high priests and the Jew's Sanhedrin who were "prosecutors" and "judges", as well as the people who shouted: "Crucify him!" It is unclear what sort of people made up the crowd. There were probably Jews who did not know much about Jesus but truly believed that he was a criminal, and there were also Jewish religious believers who felt that their religious traditions and identity were threatened because of Jesus' doctrines. There were Romans and people from other countries who did not understand what was happening, but wanted to take part anyway.

What did Jesus himself say about his mother and father, according to the sources we have available today?

In the New Testament there are only a few texts recounting about Jesus and his mother. In the gospel of Mark we read about Mary visiting Jesus when he is busy with teaching people.

"Then his brothers and his mother came, and standing outside they sent to him, calling him. And a multitude was sitting around him; and they said to him, 'Look, your mother and your brothers are outside seeking you.' But he answered them, saying, 'Who is my mother, or my brothers?' And he looked around in a circle at those who sat about him, and said, 'Here are my mother, or my brothers! For whoever does the will of God is my brother and my sister and mother.'" (Mark 4:31–35)

When reading this text, one may get the impression that Jesus was a rigid young man who hardly wanted to meet his mother and step-brothers. However, his words were certainly not aimed to reject them, but he purposed to teach the multitude what God's universal family meant. He wanted them to learn that the uniting force is spirituality and faith.

According to the author of *The Gospel of Luke,* Jesus perplexed the people once when he said: *"If anyone come to me and does not hate his father and mother, wife and children, brothers and sisters, yes, and his own life also, he cannot be my disciple." (Luke 14:26)*

There are many reasons for doubting the reliability of Luke's rendering these controversial words of Jesus. It is doubtful that the Master, who said, *"love your enemies, bless those who curse you, do good to those who hate you, and pray for those who spitefully use you and persecute you," (Matthew 5:44)*, suddenly changes his mind and starts teaching to hate one's parents and siblings. Luke's text can be either a mischievous addition inserted to discredit Jesus, or it is the result of misunderstanding the Master's teaching in Aramaic about the difference between the human's physical, biological parents and the heavenly, Spiritual Mother and Father. It is noteworthy that Luke did never listen to Jesus so we suspect that he did not know about the Master's duel opinion. According to *The Gospel of Thomas*, Jesus really made difference between the biological and eternal parents. There are many texts rendering his attachment to the heavenly Father and Mother, yet this does not mean that he underestimated his biological parents. As *The Gospel of Thomas* was in pretty bad shape when it was found, the missing words of the following text are put in brackets. We read:

"Whoever does not hate (father) and mother as I do cannot be a (disciple) of me, and whoever does (not) love (father and) mother as I do cannot be a (disciple of) me. For my mother (gave me falsehood), but my true (mother) gave me life." (Nag Hammadi Scriptures, The Gospel of Thomas, page 152)

Jesus knew that one of the most important rules of the Jewish society was to love the parents. However, he also knew that genealogical tablets and family bounds caused many problems and therefore he wanted to elevate the parenthood to a metaphysical level. According to *The Second Revelation of James*, Jesus said to his stepbrother:

"Your father is not my Father, but my Father has become a father to you. Your father, whom you consider rich, will grant that you inherit all that you see.

*But I proclaim to you
that I shall give you
what I shall say,
if you listen.
So open your ears,
and understand,
and walk accordingly …*
understand and know the Father who has compassion, who was not given an inheritance, whose inheritance is unlimited …"
(Nag Hammadi Scriptures, The Second Revelation of James, page 336 … 337)

There are unauthorized scriptures recounting Jesus' loving attitude to and feeling for Mary and Joseph. According to *The History of Joseph the Carpenter,* Jesus said:

"*Mary I called my mother, and Joseph father, and I obeyed them in all that they said; nor did I ever contend against them, but complied with their commands, as other men whom earth produces are wont to do; nor did I at any time arouse their anger, or give any word or answer in opposition to them. On the contrary,* **I cherished them with great love, like the pupil of my eye.**" (JESUS, The Unauthorised Version, Jesus' Parents, page 43)

Jesus also reports that when Joseph was "at the very point of death", and all his children lamented and mourned, he and Mary wept along with them: *"I also, and my mother Mary, wept along with them."* (The History of Joseph the Carpenter, page 46)

According to *Nicholas Notovitch's book, The Unknown Life of Jesus Christ, Chapter XII,* Jesus said:

"Hearken to what I say to you: Respect woman; for in her we see the mother of the universe, and all the truth of divine creation is to come through her.

She is the fount of everything good and beautiful, as she is also the germ of life and death. Upon her man depends in all his existence, for she is his moral and natural support in his labors.

In pain and suffering she brings you forth; in the sweat of her brow she watches over your growth, and until her death you cause her greatest anxieties. Bless her and adore her, for she is your only friend and support.

Respect her; defend her. In so doing you will gain for yourself her love; you will find favor before God, and for her sake many sins will be remitted to you.

Love your wives and respect them, for they will be the mothers of to-morrow and later the grandmothers of a whole nation.

Be submissive to the wife; her love ennobles man, softens his hardened heart, tames the wild beast in him and changes it to a lamb.

Wife and mother are priceless treasures which God has given to you. They are the most beautiful ornaments of the universe, and from them will be born all who will inhabit world.

Therefore I say unto you, after God, to woman must belong your best thoughts, for she is the divine temple where you will most easily obtain perfect happiness.

Draw from this temple your moral force. There you will forget your sorrows and your failures, and recover the love necessary to aid your fellow-men.

Suffer her not to be humiliated, for humiliating her you humiliate yourselves, and lose the sentiment of love, without which nothing can exist here on earth.

Protect your wife, that she may protect you – you and all your household. All that you do for your mothers, your wives, for a widow, or for any other woman in distress, you will do for your God." (Nicholas Notowitch's quatation from a document preserved by Buddhist monks at the Hemis convent in Tibet/Notovitch script, The Unknown Life of Jesus Christ, Chapter XII, v 10–21)

Misinterpreted and doubtful information has been delivered not only about Jesus' parents but also about **the birth of Jesus.**

Luke, the Greek doctor, for instance writes the well-known story of Jesus' being born in a stable in Bethlehem in Judea. Luke writes that all the particulars he delivers are reliable, but historical facts prove that his story is not correct. We read:

"And it came to pass in those days that a decree went out from Caesar Augustus that all the world should be registered.

This census first took place while Quirinius was governing Syria. So all went to be registered, everyone to his own city.

And Joseph also went up from Galilee, out of the city of Nazareth, into Judea, to the city of David, which is called Bethlehem, because he was of the house of lineage of David, to be registered with Mary, his bethrothed wife, who was with child.

So it was, that while they were there, the days were completed for her to be delivered.

And she brought forth her first-born son, and wrapped him in swaddling cloths, and laid him in a manger, because there was no room for them in the inn." (Luke 2:1–7)

Christian historians and theologians accept Luke's assertion that Mary and Joseph were in Judea, in the city of David, called Bethlehem when Mary gave birth to her child. However, there are several evidences that Luke's statement is wrong and that **it is more credible that Mary gave birth to her child in another Bethlehem situated in Galilee at a distance of only 11 km from Nazareth.**

Aviram Oshri, a senior archaeologist with the Israeli Antiquities Authority, asserts that there is no archaeological evidence that Bethlehem in Judea existed as a functioning town between 7 and 4 BCE when Jesus is believed to have been born. Archeological research of the town have turned up a great deal of ancient Iron Age material from 1200 to 550 BCE as well as material from the 6th century CE, but nothing has been found from the 1st century BCE or the 1st century CE.

Aviram Oshri wrote in his article *"Where was Jesus Born?* published in Archeology magazine, Volume 58 Number 6, 2005:

"I have never before questioned the assumption that Jesus was born in Bethlehem in Judea. But in the early 1990s, as an archaeologist working for the IAA, I was contracted to perform some salvage excavations around building and infrastructure projects in a small rural community in the Galilee. When I started work, some of the people who lived around the site told me that Jesus was really born there, not in the south. Intrigued,

I researched the archaeological evidence for Bethlehem in Judea at the time of Jesus and found nothing. This is very surprising, as Herodian remains should be the first thing one should find. What was even more surprising is what archeologists had already uncovered and what I was to discover over the next 11 years of excavation at the small rural site – Bethlehem of Galilee." (source of the quotation: (www.archaeology.org/)

As excavations in Bethlehem in Galilee between 1992 and 2003 have uncovered the remains of the largest Christian Church and monastery in Israel, built circa 4th or 5th century, Aviram Oshri concludes: *"There is no doubt in my mind that these are impressive and important evidence of a strong Christian community established in Bethlehem …"* Oshri is certain that the church is Christian because they also found oil lamps with cross, baptismal font and bronze cross. He also asserts that Christians would have not been motivated to build such a big church in Bethlehem in Galilee, if they had not known that Jesus was born there.

Oshri says that Christian ecclesiastics and other authorities do not want to recognize Bethlehem in Galilee as the birthplace of Jesus because "Business interests are too important".

"The Christmas story" according to Luke may be doubted for many other reasons.

Physicians say that a heavily pregnant woman, as Mary was, would have not been able to ride a donkey ca 150 km without losing her baby.

Historians say that, even if Joseph had been required to register with the authorities in Bethlehem in Judea, Mary would have not traveled with him as women did not need to be registered and besides Mary did not originate from Judea.

Luke writes that Quirinius was governor when Jesus was born, but this is not correct either as he was appointed as a governor of Syria in 6 CE when Jesus was aged about 6 or 10.

Luke also states that *"in those days a decree went out from Caesar Augustus that all the world should be registered,"* but actually there was no single census of the entire empire under Caesar Augustus.

Besides, no Roman census required people to travel from their homes back to the place of distant ancestors. The Roman Empire consisted of a mixed population coming from many different regions of the empire, from the most remote areas in Africa, Spain, Britain, Asia Minor etc., so it had been impossible to require people to travel back to the place of their ancestors.

What do we know about **the adolescent Jesus?**

Unfortunately, there is only one text in the New Testament that gives some information about the adolescent Jesus. According to the author of The Gospel of Luke, Jesus is 12 years old when he travels to Jerusalem with the parents to celebrate the Feast of the Passover. When the Feast is over and the parents together with their relatives and acquaintances are on the way back to Galilee, Jesus is not with them and that is why Mary and Joseph have to return to Jerusalem to seek him. They find him "in the temple, sitting in the midst of the teachers, both listening to them and asking them questions."

"And when he was twelve years old, they went up to Jerusalem according to the custom of the feast. When they had finished the days, as they returned, the boy Jesus lingered behind in Jerusalem. And Joseph and his mother did not know it;

but supposing him to have been in the company, they went a day's journey, and sought him among their relatives and acquaintances.

So when they did not find him, they returned to Jerusalem, seeking him.

Now so it was after three days they found him in the temple, sitting in the midst of the teachers, both listening to them and asking them questions.

And all who heard him were astonished at his understanding and answers.

So when they saw him, they were amazed; and his mother said to him, 'Son, why have you done this to us? Look, your father and I have sought you anxiously.'

And he said to them, 'Why is it that you sought me? Did you not know that I must be about my Father's business?'

But they did not understand the words which he spoke to them." (Luke 2:42–50)

After this incident in Jerusalem, there is no more information in the New Testament about what Jesus did the period following until he starts spreading his doctrines. "He was a carpenter, and worked in Joseph's workshop", assert the ecclesiastics of the institutional church without having any confirmation in writing. On the contrary, their statement is contradicted by ancient scrolls, preserved in distant countries, in India and Tibet. According to documents that have been found in the Himis monastery in Tibet, Jesus was a *"meditative youth, whose mind was far above anything corporeal, and possessed by the thirst for knowledge; he joined the caravans going to India, where he began to frequent the temple of Djainites ... In sympathetic admiration for the spirit of the young man, the Djainites asked him to stay with them, but Jesus left them to settle in Djagguernat, where he studied the religion of Brahmins.*

... ...

Jesus spent six years in Djagguernat in studying the language of the country and the Sanscrit, which enabled him to study the religions, doctrines, philosophy, medicine and mathematics.

He found much to blame in Brahmanical laws and usages.

The Brahmins tried in vain to convince him of the sacred character of their established religious customs.

Jesus denied the existence of all hierarchical gods the Brahmins believed in *and thought about.*

When **the Brahmins** *saw that Jesus turned out to be their adversary and that the people began to embrace his doctrine, they* **resolved to kill him and his servants** ...

Jesus took refuge in the mountains of Nepal.

Jesus stayed six-years among the Buddhists, *where he found the principle of monotheism.*

When he was 26, he decided to turn back to his homeland. On his way homeward, he preached against idol-ship, human sacrifice, and other errors of faith, admonishing people to believe in God, the Father of all beings, to whom all are dear alike." (Nicholas Notovitch, The Unknown Life of Jesus Christ)

When the Russian doctor **Nicholas Notovitch** (1858–after 1916) journeyed throughout Afghanistan, India and Tibet in order to do his own researches, he got surprising information about Jesus in a Buddhist convent.

During his journey down into the arid rocky land of Ladak Notovitch had an accident and his leg was broken, so he had to stay for a time at the Himis convent.

While he was there, he learned that there existed ancient records of the life of Jesus. A Buddhist monk showed him two large yellowed volumes containing the biography of *Jesus* who was called St. *Issa* in Asia.

Notovitch enlisted a member of his party to translate the scrolls that he took to Russia when he turned back to his homeland where there was much controversy concerning the script. As the scrolls contained information about **Jesus visiting India and Tibet before and after the crucifixion,** Notovitch was accused of creating a hoax and was ridiculed as an imposter. In his defense he encouraged a scientific expedition to prove that the original Tibetan documents really existed. He even contacted Cardinal Rotelli in Rome and handed him over the translated scripts hoping that the Vatican would start a research.

Later Notovitch sustained that in the library of the Vatican there were 63 documents originating from Asia about Jesus and his disciple Thomas who stayed in India.

One of the skeptics who doubted Notovitch's discovery about Jesus' life in Asia, was **Swami Abhedananda** (1866–1939), author, journalist, philosopher and head of the Vedanta Society of New York. He journeyed to India and in 1922 he crossed the Himalayas on foot and reached Tibet, where he studied Buddhist philosophy and Lamaism. He also visited the Himis monastery and concluded that the scrolls reporting *the lost years of Jesus,* really existed, so Notovitch was not an impostor. The lamas at the monastery confirmed to him that Notovitch was indeed brought to the monastery with a broken leg and he was nursed there for a month and a half. They told him that the manuscript on Jesus had been shown to Notovitch and contents interpreted.

Swami also got some portions of the manuscript (about 40 verses) translated with the help of a lama. Swami was surprised to hear that Jesus came secretly to Kashmir after the crucifixion and later had many disciples. The monks said that the original manuscript in Pali was written "three or four years" after Issa's death, on the basis of reports by local Tibetans who often listened to Issa's teachings and on the basis of accounts from wandering Jewish merchants who also had had contact with Jesus living in Kashmir/Shrinagar after the crucifixion.

In 1925 another Russian named **Nicholas Roerich** arrived to Himis. He was a philosopher, a distinguished scientist and artist. He recorded in his own travel diary the same information N. Notovitch and S. Abhedananda reported about Jesus'/Issa' life in Asia.

Nicholas Roerich wrote in his travel diary, *Altai-Himalaya*:

"Issa said that man had filled the temples with abominations. In order to pay homage to metals and stones (statues), man sacrificed his fellows in whom dwells a spark of the Supreme Spirit."

N. Roerich also reports that Jesus/Issa said to the Brahma priests – Vaishas and Shudras, *"Worship not the idols. Do not consider yourself first. Do not humiliate your neighbor. Help the poor. Sustain the feeble. Do evil to no one …"*

N. Roerich was very impressed of what he had learned about Jesus/Issa whom the lamas and Buddhists even called as "The Healer of Leprous" and whom common people considered to be their "buddha". N. Roerich writes about a Hindu putting the following questions: *"Why does one always place Issa in Egypt during the time of his absence from Palestine? … And why does one not see traces of Buddhism- of India? It is difficult to understand why the wandering of Issa by caravan path into India and into the region now occupied by Tibet, should be so vehemently denied."*

Presumably, Jesus did not only study the Brahman Vedanta and the doctrines of Buddhism, but he attained loads of knowledge about Greek philosophy, Taoism and Confucianism as well as the mysteries of Egypt religion.

It is said that on his way back to his homeland, he spent some time in Egypt where he attended Mystery Schools. When he turns back to Galilee and starts healing people, some Jews call him "the magician from Egypt".

The uncommon method of healing people as well as Jesus' new doctrines about *The One, Who Is the Light and the Supreme Invisible Spirit* scared the Jewish religious leaders, the Pharisees and the scribes as the Master had a big impact on people listening to him, so they decided to get rid of him.

"And the chief priests and the scribes sought how they might take him by trickery and put him to death." (Mark 14:1)

DID JESUS DIE ON THE CROSS?

Before Crucifixion

The chief priests, Pharisees and scribes accused Jesus for being a "deceiver" of the ancestors' religious traditions. They did not understand that Jesus did not want to deceive the religion of the ancestors, but he wanted to reform the pagan tradition of offering animals in the temple of Jerusalem as well as he wanted to stop the Jew's believing in a Lord who encourages war. The priests of the Jerusalem temple did not understand that Jesus drove out the temple money-changers and merchants selling animals to be offered because he wanted to establish a temple where the heathen ritual of offering animals should be changed to spirituality and genuine faith. The priests of Jerusalem temple, who wanted to keep the traditions of the ancestors, were for certain upset when Jesus *"found in the temple those who sold oxen and sheep and doves"* that should be offered on the altar of the temple. *"When he had made a whip of cords, he drove them all out of the temple, with the sheep and the oxen, and poured out the coins of the money-changers and overturned the tables. And he said to those who sold doves, 'Take these things away! Do not make my Father's house a house of merchandise!'"* (John 2:14 … 16)

Jesus wanted to reform not only the religion of the Jews, but he also combated polytheist religions in the Far East, like Hinduism as well as the idolatry of the multitude of gods in Egypt. According to documents written in the first century and preserved by Buddhist monks in India, Jesus said to a Magi in India:

"'Your doctrine is the fruit of your error in seeking to bring near to you the God of Truth, by creating for yourselves false gods.'

When the Magi heard these words, they feared to themselves do him harm, but at night, when the whole city slept, they brought him outside the walls and left him on the highway, in the hope that he would not fail to become the prey of wild beasts.

But, protected by the Lord our God, Saint Issa continued on his way, without accident." (Notovitch, The Unknown Life of Jesus Christ: The Life of Saint Issa: VIII, v. 222–24)

Jesus' life was many times in danger while fulfilling his mission in India and Egypt, but he did not fear death and suffering. According to *The Secret Book of James*, Jesus appeared after his crucifixion and had a dialogue with Peter and James about the dangers and sufferings he had had to bear. He said:

"'Don't you know that you have not yet been abused, unjustly accused, locked up in prison, unlawfully condemned, crucified without reason, or buried in the sand as I myself was by the evil one? … Remember my cross …'

I (James) answered and said to him, 'Master, do not mention to us the cross and death, for they are far from you.'"

(Nag Hammadi Scriptures, The Secret Book of James, "Believe in My Cross" (4,22 … 6,21, page 25 … 26)

As burial in sand was characteristic in Egypt, we assume that Jesus talks about an experience he had in Egypt before turning back to Galilee and Judea where later some Jewish religious leaders call him "the magic from Egypt".

The Crucifixion

Thanks to new archeological discoveries as well as non-biblical scripts many new information about Jesus' life and death has been revealed; however, the most striking "good news" is that Jesus did not die on the cross but was rescued. This statement surprises Christians generally and startles ecclesiastics. The great majority of the Christians wonders: "Can this be true?" "Have the doctrines of the institutional Church about Jesus' death and resurrection been wrong?"

Mr. Samuelsson, theologian of Gothenburg (Sweden) University said:

"The text of the passion narratives is not that exact and information loaded, as we Christians sometimes want it to be."

"We should read the text as it is, not as we think it is. We should read the lines, not between the lines. The text of the Bible is sufficient."

The Bible really delivers a lot of information about the passion history, but, as the jigsaws of the story are sometimes controversial, there are many unsolved questions concerning the crucifixion of Jesus.

"Was Jesus or somebody else bearing the cross to Golgotha?" is, for instance, a controversial question that can be answered both "yes" or "no", depending which gospel we read. According to the authors of The Gospel of Matthew, Luke and Mark, it was not Jesus who was bearing the cross, while the author of The Gospel of John writes that the Master, who had suffered physical injuries when being judged, had to bear the cross. We read in the Gospel of Luke:

"Now as they led him (Jesus) away, they laid hold of a certain man, **Simon a Cyrenian,** *who was coming from the country,* **and on him they laid the cross that he might bear it after Jesus.**

And a great multitude of the people followed him, and women who also mourned and lamented him." (Luke 23:26–27)

If this information is correct, we can conclude that there were people who wanted to help the Master in his great pain and suffering already on his way to Golgotha.

According to literary sources, people condemned to crucifixion never carried the complete cross, that was well over 135 kg. Only the crossbar was carried, while the upright set was in a permanent place and it was used for subsequent executions.

At the site of execution, by law, the victim was given **a drink as a mild pain reliever.** The gospels supply different information concerning the drink Jesus was offered when he was crucified. The author of *The Gospel of Matthew* writes, that *"they gave him **sour wine mingled with gall** to drink. But when he had tasted it, he would not drink it."(Matthew 27:34)*

In *The Gospel of Mark* we read that *"they gave him **wine mingled with myrrh** to drink, but he did not take it." (Mark 15:23)*

The second drink Jesus is offered after having been on the cross a few hours, was *sour wine*, according all the gospels of the New Testament.

"Now a vessel full of sour wine was sitting there; and they filled a sponge with sour wine, put it on hyssop, and put it to his mouth.

*So **when Jesus had received the sour wine, he said, 'It is finished!'** And bowing his head, he gave up his spirit." (John 19:29–30)*

The perfect timing of Jesus "giving up his spirit" when he gets a sponge filled with sour wine to his mouth, suggests that maybe his fainting was not a mere chance. Thanks to this act the soldiers, who were breaking the legs of the crucified ones, get the impression that Jesus is already dead, so they do not break his legs. But, at the same time another soldier does something remarkable: he pierces Jesus side with a spear even if he thinks that he is dead. The question is why to pierce the side of a man already dead?

"Then the soldiers came and broke the legs of the first and of the other who was crucified with him.

But when they came to Jesus and saw that he was already dead, they did not break his legs.
But one of the soldiers pierced his side with a spear, and immediately blood and water came out." (John 19:32–34)

There are many speculations concerning the special treatment of Jesus compared to the other two men who were crucified at the same time with him. Several researchers assume that the drink on the sponge, the "non-breaking of his legs" and the piercing of Jesus' side were bribed actions that Joseph of Arimathea, Nicodemus or some other friends of Jesus had fixed in order to help him to survive the crucifixion.

There are different theories concerning the piercing of Jesus' side. Experts think that the piercing was not a spontaneous action of the soldier, but it was arranged by Jesus' friends with the intention to prevent his death by asphyxiation.

Dr. Muhammad Masudul Hasan Nuri, of the Tahir Heart Institute, tries to explain how it is possible that Jesus survived the crucifixion. He points out that the average length of stay on the crucifix before death used to be three days, and that Jesus was taken off the cross after a few hours the same day he was crucified. Dr. Nuri confirms that the soldier who pierced the side of Jesus, helped the Master not to be asphyxiated. Dr. Nuri says that "the flow of blood and water was helpful to respiration and beneficial in the renewing life." This is a well-known medical practice in case of patients with cardiac tampomade (bleeding within the pericardial cavity) where after aspiration with a wide bore needle the blood is allowed to drain to avoid recollection."

The author of The Gospel of Mark recounts that, when Pilate was asked for permission to take off the body of Jesus from the cross, he was surprised that Jesus was already dead:

"Now when evening had come, because it was the Preparation Day, that is, the day before the Sabbath,

> *Joseph of Arimathea, a prominent council member, who also waited for the kingdom of God, came and went in boldly to Pilate and asked for the body of Jesus.*
>
> **Pilate marveled that he was already dead;** *and summoning the centurion, he asked him if he had been dead for some time." (Mark 15:42–44)*

Why did Pilate "marvel" when hearing that Jesus was dead after a few hours hanging on the cross? Why did the chief priests and Pharisees insist at all that Jesus should be crucified the day before the Passover when they knew that the crucified persons generally were kept on the cross about three days, but according to Jewish law and tradition, there should nobody be hanging on the cross during the Feast? What was the plan of the chief priests, of Caiaphas and the Sanhedrin when pushing Pilate to take a quick decision the day before the Feast? Did they only want to bring shame upon Jesus for not having respected the Jewish religious traditions of the ancestors? As in Persia and the Roman Empire the crucifixion was used to punish traitors, rebels, robbers and criminal slaves, one may suspect that the Pharisees and chief priests purposed to humiliate Jesus. They also wanted probably to prove to the Jews that he was not a beloved of God. If killing Jesus had been their only purpose, then they could have paid more money to Judah or someone else to kill him secretly or they could have waited until the Passover was over.

According to *The Gospel of Mark,* even Jesus was surprised when *"a great multitude with swords and clubs came from the chief priests and the scribes and the elders"* in order to arrest him in Gethsemane. He said to them: *"Have you come out, as against a robber, with swords and clubs to take me? I was daily with you in the temple teaching, and you did not take me." (Mark 14:48–49)*

It is evident that the Jewish religious leaders wanted to have a show up there and at that time of Passover when there were thousands of Jews from different countries and parts of the Roman Empire who had come to Jerusalem to celebrate. Probably there had been rumors about Jesus' new doctrines even among Jews living abroad, so Rabies and chief priests from different countries wanted the Jerusalem Sanhedrin to take measurements.

According to **The Gospel of Matthew,** *"about the ninth hour Jesus cried out with a loud voice, saying, 'Eli, Eli, lama sabachtani?' that is,* **'My God, my God, why have you forsaken me?'"** *(Matthew 27:46)* It is doubtful that Jesus, who did not talk Hebrew but Aramaic, should on the cross use words from Psalm 22:1 in Hebrew to express his disappointment and to complain that God has forsaken him. The text in The Gospel of Matthew is probably a spontaneous addition of the author who frequently quotes The Old Testament using words and quotations as if they were Jesus' words. It even can be a later addition of an editor who wanted to insinuate that Jesus deserved to be abandoned by the God of Israel, as he was a renegade of the Jewish religious traditions.

The author of **The Gospel of Luke** recounts other words of the Master crying out before being unconscious: *"when Jesus had cried out with a loud voice, he said,* **'Father, into your hands I commend my spirit.** *'And having said this, he breathed his last." (Luke 23:46)*

As the language Jesus talked was Aramaic, it is more credible that he cried out in his mother tongue: *"Eli, Eli – Lama Sabag Ta-Nim!"*, that means *"God, God! Lift up the lacerate one into Your Eternal Wholeness!"* These words in Aramaic sound quite similar to the Hebrew Psalm verse, *"Eli, Eli, lama sabachtani,"* quoted by the author of The Gospel of Matthew. However, theologically there is a very essential difference between the two interpretations of the so called "Jesus' last words on the cross". According to The Gospel of Matthew Jesus complained and mistrusted God instead of praying trustfully for help, as the Aramaic text suggests.

The crowed who wanted to see the execution, including the woman-disciples of Jesus, were not allowed to come close to the cross, so it is doubtful that any of the gospel authors has reported the right "last words" of Jesus. The Roman soldiers who were the executors of the crucifixion, did probably not understand Aramaic or Hebrew, so they were not able to report later any last words of the Master.

The Empty Tomb

We read in the Gospel of John:
*"Joseph of Arimathea came and took the body of Jesus. And **Nicodemus**, who at first came to Jesus by night, also **came, bringing a mixture of myrrh and aloes, about a hundred pounds.***

Then they took the body of Jesus, and bound it in strips of linen with the spices, as the custom of the Jews is in burying.

Now in the place where he was crucified there was a garden, and in the garden a new tomb in which no one had yet been laid." (John 19:38 … 40)

Why did Nicodemus come with about 30 kg mixture of myrrh and aloe? – is an important question, as, the general Jewish burial tradition does not motivate that big quantity of myrrh and aloe. Embalming was practiced in Egypt and Rome, and was almost unknown in Jewish tradition, or at least exceedingly rare in Judea. Actually, nothing is mentioned about "embalming" Jesus' body either; we only read that his body was bound in "strips of linen with the spices". In order to remove the odor and avoid the rapid decomposition that occurred in the Mediterranean heat, spices, that is aromatic herbs as aloe oil, laurel, palm and cypress were put on the coffin or in the water with which the dead was washed. But washing the body of the dead is a later practice and it is not mentioned in Jesus'case either.

Taking into account the Jewish burial traditions, Nicodemus did not need to come with about 30 kg mixture of myrrh and aloe. His purpose with the mixture was probably to prevent infection of Jesus' wounds and as well as to help his recovering.

If we take into consideration the amazing benefits of myrrh and aloe, then we will understand why Nicodemus hoped he could heal Jesus. **Myrrh** is antimicrobial, astringent, expectorant, stimulant, circulatory, anti-inflammatory and it even has antispasmodic properties. In ancient Egypt, Greece and other lands the oil obtained from myrrh was used for healing wounds, and preventing infection of wounds. Myrrh also stops hemorrhaging in wounds, as it makes the blood vessels contract.

Aloe is used as a remedy for skin conditions and wounds including cold sores, as well as for treating bowel diseases, fever, itching and inflammation.

Jesus' friends, first of all Nicodemus and Joseph of Arimathea probably knew that the Master was not dead, so they wanted to help him to recover from the injuries as soon as possible. They also knew that, according to Jewish burial tradition, the tomb needed not to be immediately closed over the dead. During the first three days it was customary for the relatives to visit the grave to see whether the dead had come to life again, as quick burials involved the danger of entombing persons alive. The gospels report that Joseph of Arimathea rolled a stone against the door of the tomb which means that he could roll away the stone whenever he wanted.

Only the author of The Gospel of Matthew writes that *"On the next day, which followed the Day of Preparation, the chief priests and Pharisees gathered together to Pilate, saying, 'Sir, we remember, while he was alive, how the deceiver said, 'After three days I will rise.'*

Therefore command that the tomb be made secure until the third day, lest his disciples should come by night and steal him away …

Pilate said to them, 'You have a guard; go your way, make it as secure as you know how.'

So they went and made the tomb secure, sealing the stone and setting the guard." (Matthew 27:2 ... 66)

One of the reasons to question the validity of this text is that the other evangelists Mark, Luke, John or other scripts do not mention anything about the chief priests going to Pilate on the day of Passover. On that special Feast day the Jews and the chief priests should not do any other activities but celebrating and praying. Besides, the tomb had not been sealed and guarded the night before, so why would they have bothered to put a guard one day later?

The author of the Gospel of Matthew reports that there was "a great earthquake" when an angel descended from heaven to roll back the stone from the door. We read: *"there was a great earthquake; for an angel of the Lord descended from heaven, and came and rolled back the stone from the door"* (Matthew 28:1 ... 2)

There are no other texts in the Bible or in other scripts, history books for instance, informing about a great earthquake in Jerusalem early in the morning that day. Had it really occurred, then it had been mentioned as a big sign or catastrophe. Besides, the women who came to the tomb, did not report either of any earthquake or of a guard being there. Actually, the women who had come with Jesus from Galilee, followed after when the Master's body was taken to the tomb and "observed the tomb and how his body was laid". They decided to go to the tomb early in the morning after Passover, as they knew that there was no guard there; their only concern was how to roll away the stone that Joseph of Arimathea had rolled to the entrance of the tomb.

Mary and *"other women who had come with him (Jesus) from Galilee, followed after, and they observed the tomb and how his body was laid.*

Then they returned and prepared spices and fragrant oils. And they rested on the Sabbath according to the commandment.

> *Now on the first day of the week, very early in the morning, they, and certain other women with them, came to the tomb bringing the spices which they had prepared.*
> *But **they found the stone rolled away** from the tomb.*
> *Then they went in and **did not find the body of the Lord Jesus**." (Luke 23:55–56, 24:1–3)*

Later theologians and ecclesiastics use the story of the empty tomb when formulating the dogma according to which Christ resurrected in his physical body. It is astonishing that they never doubt that their argument is absurd.

Jesus Meets the Disciples After the Crucifixion

The disciples who had experienced Jesus' special abilities and teachings during the years they followed him were scared and surprised when the Master was arrested and put on the cross. However, they were much more surprised when they saw the Master again after the crucifixion. There are reports about Jesus' contacting the disciples both in his physical body, when he eats and drinks and does things with them, as well as about his appearing as a celestial being that the disciples recognize only when the Master starts a dialogue with them. It is noteworthy that when Jesus appeared in his "spirit figure", a bright light shining around him is always mentioned, but nothing is said about the light when the Master meets them in his physical body.

In *The Secret Book of John* we read that Jesus appeared to John who, being distressed after the crucifixion went to a mountainous and barren place and thought on questions concerning Jesus:

*"I was distressed within, and I asked how the Savior was chosen:
Why was he sent into the world by his Father?
Who is his Father who sent him?
To what kind of eternal realm shall we go? …*

At the moment I was thinking about this, look, the heavens opened, all creation under heaven lit up

I was afraid, and look, I saw within the light someone standing by me. As I was looking, it seemed to be an elderly person. Again it changed its appearance to be a youth. Not that there were several figures before me. Rather, there was a figure with several forms within the light. These forms were visible through each other, and the figure had three forms.

The figure said to me, 'John, John, why are you doubting? Why are you afraid? Aren't you familiar with this figure? Then do not be fainthearted. I am with you always. I am the Father, I am the Mother, I am the Child. I am the incorruptible and the undefiled one. Now I have come to teach you what is, what was, and what is going to come, that you may understand what is invisible and what is visible;'" (NG, The Secret Book of John, The Revealer Appears to John 1,5 … 2,25, page 107–108)

The vision of "a figure with several forms" scared John as he could not even imagine such a phenomenon before. We do not know what Jesus' purpose was when he appeared both as a young and as an old man. We only guess that he wanted to show John sequences of his life even showing himself to grow old. "I have come to teach you what is, what was, and what is going to come", he says. To teach "what is" may be interpreted that Jesus wanted to show John that he was alive even if that moment he appeared to him as a celestial being. Jesus knows that John has already experienced his double nature several times before, and that is why he says to him *"John, John, why are you doubting? Why are you afraid? Aren't you familiar with this figure?"*.

After the crucifixion Jesus probably appeared in his bilocated figure to Mary Magdalene who was weeping at the empty tomb.

"But Mary stood outside by the tomb weeping, and as she wept she stooped down and looked into the tomb.

And she saw two angels in white sitting, one at the head and the other at the feet, where the body of Jesus had lain.

Then they said to her, 'Woman, why are you weeping?' She said to them, 'Because they have taken away my Lord, and I do not know where they have laid him.'

Now when she had said this, she turned around and saw Jesus standing there, and did not know that it was Jesus.

Jesus said to her, 'Woman, why are you weeping? Whom are you seeking?'

She, supposing him to be the gardener, said to him, 'Sir, if you have carried him away, tell me where you have laid him, and I will take him away.'

Jesus said to her, 'Mary!' She turned and said to him, 'Rabboni!' (which is to say, Teacher).

Jesus said to her, 'Do not cling to me, for I have not yet ascended to my Father;'" (John 20:11–17)

Jesus's declaration "*I have not yet ascended to my Father*" contradicts the assertion in The Apostles Creed that "*on the third day he ascended into heaven*". The next text, reporting Jesus' coming to the disciples in the evening, as well as many other texts rendering the Master's meeting the disciples, suggests that Jesus did not ascend to the Father after the crucifixion as he was not yet "clinically dead"; very likely, while some disciples were healing his tortured body, he bilocated and showed himself to the distressed Mary whom he wanted to comfort by giving her a sign that he was alive. He did the same thing in the evening when he suddenly appeared to the disciples.

"Then, the same day at evening, being the first day of the week, when the doors were shut where the disciples were assembled, for fear of the Jews, Jesus came and stood in the midst, and said to them, 'Peace be with you.'

Now when he had said this, he showed them his hands and his side.

Then the disciples were glad when they saw the Lord." (John 20:19–20)

The author of The Gospel of Mark writes that the women entering the tomb, *"saw a young man clothed in a long white robe"* who said them to go and tell the disciples that Jesus is going before them to Galilee where they will see him, as he had told them. There are several texts documenting that the Master really met them in Galilee later, after his recovering. But before leaving for Galilee, Jesus met his stepbrother, James who reports that people "were waiting for the sign of his coming, and it came after some days."

"They were waiting for the sign of his coming, and it came after some days. James was walking on the mountain called Gaugela (note: perhaps Golgotha; in Syriac, Gagultha) *along with his disciples, who still listened to him with desire. They had a comforter, and they said, 'This is the second teacher.' The crowd dispersed, but James remained behind and prayed …, as was his custom.*

The master appeared to him. He stopped praying, embraced him, and kissed him, saying: 'Rabbi, I've found you. I heard of the sufferings you endured, and I was greatly troubled.' (NG, The First Revelation of James 30,16 … 32,28, page 327)

The author of The Gospel of Matthew also mentions that an angel said to the women: "*Do not be afraid, for I know that you seek Jesus who was crucified.*

He is not here; for he is risen, as he said …

Go quickly and tell his disciples that he is risen from the dead, and indeed **he is going before you into Galilee; there you will see him**." *(Matthew 28:5 … 7)*

"*And as they went to tell his disciples, behold,* **Jesus met them**, *saying, 'Rejoice!'"* **And they came and held him by the feet and worshiped him**.

Then Jesus said to them, 'Do not be afraid. **Go and tell my brethren to go to Galilee, and there they will see me**.' *(Matthew 28:9–10)*

"Then **the eleven disciples went away into Galilee**, *to the mountain which Jesus had appointed for them.*

*And when **they saw him**, they worshiped him; but some doubted." (Matthew 28:16–17)*

These texts need no comments as they clearly suggest that Jesus was alive after the crucifixion and planned to meet the disciples in Galilee where he later carried on teaching them. But, according to *The Gospel of Nicodemus (Acts of Pilate)*, his staying in Galilee was not safe as it was soon reported to the chief priests in Jerusalem who then sent people there to find him. Three men came down of Galilee to Jerusalem and they said with an oath:

"We saw Jesus upon the mount Mamilch with his disciples and he taught them all things." (From The Apocryphal New Testament, M.R. James-Translation, Oxford: Clarendon Press, 1924)

These men also assert that they saw Jesus being *"taken up into heaven"*, but *"no man asked them in what manner he was taken up."* According to The Gospel of Nicodemus, the chief priests sent people to seek out Jesus on the mountains, but nobody could find him. They found instead Joseph of Arimathea whom they arrested as they wanted to punish him for helping Jesus. But Joseph escaped the prison thanks to Jesus' miraculous help.

The Ascension of Jesus is officially celebrated even today on the 40th day of Easter when Christians commemorate the bodily ascension of Jesus into heaven, as it is written in Luke 24:50–51, as well as in The Acts 1:1–11.

According to The Acts, after the crucifixion *"Jesus began both to do and teach, until the day in which he was taken up, after he through the Holy Spirit had given commandments to the apostles whom he had chosen, to whom **he also presented himself alive after his suffering by many infallible proofs, being seen by them during forty days** and speaking of the things pertaining to the kingdom of God." (The Acts 1:1–3)*

Sceptics as well as ecclesiastics, who do not want to accept the idea of Jesus surviving the crucifixion, say that Jesus was walking around, acting and teaching in his "resurrected body". But nobody knows what they mean with a "resurrected body" walking around, eating and acting like a person alive. Surprisingly, theologians do not take into account all the texts recounting that Jesus actually recovered after the crucifixion and met the disciples again. They neglect for instance that the author of The Acts1: 1–3 says that Jesus presented himself "alive after his suffering". We also read in the Acts that Paul was arrested in Caesarea because he affirmed that Jesus, who had died, was alive. Festus, who should judge Paul, reported to King Agrippa:

"When the accusers stood up, they brought no accusation against him of such things as I supposed, but had some questions against him about their own religion and about one, Jesus, who had died, whom Paul affirmed to be alive." (Acts 25:13 … 19)

If Paul had affirmed that Jesus, who had died, was resurrected and was in heaven, then the Jews would have not accused him as they too believed in life after death. Festus reports that the accusers were upset because Paul affirmed that Jesus was alive.

There are different speculations and interpretations of what in reality happened when people saw Jesus' ascending in the heaven. One of the theories is that Jesus possessed the levitation ability and the story about Jesus' ascending in heaven renders his showing up this phenomenon.

Levitation is a well-known phenomenon which is referred to in many cases when saints ascending their physical body, levitated a short time.

It is recounted for example that Gautama Buddha "walked on water" levitating with crossed legs. Jesus also "walks on water" to meet his disciples who were in a boat.

Saint Francis of Assisi is recorded as having been "suspended above earth" often to a height of about 1,3 to 1,8 meters.

Saint Alphonsus Ligouri (1696–1787), Catholic bishop was lifted before the eyes of the whole congregation several feet from the ground, when preaching at Foggia.

Even if the list of people possessing the ability of levitation is long, nobody can prove what happened on the mountain where people saw Jesus ascending in the heaven, so the "ascension" will be one of the unsolved mysteries of Jesus. However, it is noteworthy that levitation (from Latin *levitas*, "lightness) is a phenomenon known and used in scientific techniques too. Technically, levitation is accomplished by providing an upward force that counteracts the pull of gravity. Scientists talk about and work with magnetic, electrostatic, aerodynamic, acoustic, optical and other forms of levitation.

The traditional Christian theology claims that Jesus died as an "Offer Lamb" on the cross without taking into account texts that contradict this statement. There are several biblical as well as other scripts describing Jesus eating, drinking and walking with the disciples after the crucifixion. Believing that he performed all these activities in a resurrected "spirit body", is unrealistic.

At first the disciples are perplexed and scared when Jesus presents himself, and they think that he is "a spirit". The Master understands their skepticism and fear and helps them to overcome their doubts:

"Jesus himself stood in the midst of them, and said to them, 'Peace to you.'

But **they were terrified and frightened, and supposed they had seen a spirit.**

And he said to them, 'Why are you troubled? And why do doubts arise in your hearts?

'Behold my hands and my feet, that it is I myself. Handle me and see, for a spirit does not have flesh and bones as you see I have.'

When he had said this, he showed them his hands and his feet.

But while they still did not believe for joy, and marvelled, he said to them,

'Have you any food here?'

So they gave him a piece of a broiled fish and some honeycomb. And he took it and ate in their presence" (Luke 24:36–43)

Jesus' saying that *"a spirit does not have flesh and bones"* makes obvious that the Christian dogma of 'the resurrection of flesh', formulated in The Apostles' Creed, is not correct. Church fathers and theologians editing The Apostles Creed, do not share Jesus' opinion about death, but they follow the pattern of the Jewish theology according to which there will be a physical resurrection at the end of time. The Jews have to believe what Ezekiel, the prophet says about 'the resurrection' of dry bones of dead people. We read:

"And he said to me: 'Son of man, can these bones live?' So I answered, 'LORD GOD, you know.'

Again he said to me, 'Prophesy to these bones, and say to them, 'O dry bones, hear the word of the LORD!

'Thus says the Lord God to these bones: 'Surely I will cause breath to enter into you, and you shall live.

I will put sinews on you and bring flesh upon you, cover you with skin and put breath in you; and you shall live. Then you shall know that I am the LORD." (Ezekiel 37:1 … 6)

The author of The Gospel of Matthew applies this text on events occurring when Jesus is crucified. We read in the gospel a strange and absurd story according to which, when Jesus "yielded up his spirit", *"… the earth quaked, and the rocks were split, and the graves were opened; and many bodies of the saints who had fallen asleep were raised; and coming out of the graves after his resurrection, they went into the holy city and appeared to many." (Matthew 27:51–53)*

Other gospel-authors, Luke, Mark and John do not mention anything about such a dramatic event. They do not write about opened graves and people being raised from dead and then running around in Jerusalem. If it had really happened as Matthew reports, than it had been mentioned in many scripts as a big sensation.

Tertullianus (ca 155-ca 240 AD), a prolific Christian author, believed in the resurrection of the flesh with sinews and blood vessels. He wrote that *"Without true incarnation, there can be no true redemption ... God must have flesh, in order to have real death and real resurrection." (De Carne Christ)* One may wonder which God "must have flesh"? Surely not The One Supreme Being Jesus talked about.

Church fathers formulating the Apostles' Creed took over Tertullianus' absurd thinking of the resurrection of flesh and did not taken into consideration that besides Jesus, even Paul asserts that *"flesh and blood cannot inherit the kingdom of God; nor does corruption inherit incorruption,*

Behold, I tell you a mystery: **We shall not all sleep, but we shall all be changed."** *(1 Cor. 15:50–51)*

According to *The Secret Book of James,* Jesus said to the disciples: *"'I tell you the truth, no one will ever enter heaven's kingdom because I ordered it, but rather because you yourselves are filled. Leave James and Peter to me that I may fill them.'" (NH, The Secret Book of James 2,7, page 24)* This declaration of Jesus proves that his view of salvation differs from what Christian dogmatic theologians teach. He does not say "you will enter heaven's kingdom because I will offer my life", but he talks about the power of the spirit that helps people to ascend to eternal life and he even admonishes the disciples to be filled with this power. According to John 6:63, Jesus declared that **"It is the Spirit who gives life; the flesh profits nothing".** There are many other texts evidencing that he always talked about soul/spirit when teaching about eternal life.

Unfortunately, church fathers in the past and ecclesiastics today, have preferred **Tertullianus' absurd "flesh theology"**, turning down the beautiful doctrines of Jesus presented in the New Testament and several texts of The Nag Hammadi Scriptures. Tertullianus defended "the flesh" and maintained that in the order of creation, the human flesh was prior to the soul. He called people believing in the resurrection of the soul "heretics". Theologians coming after Tertullianus were, and still are "bewitched" by the **"flesh theology" that is summarized in The Apostles Creed**. Christians have to agree with and say in the rite *"I believe in … the resurrection of the body".*

Millions of Christians have to learn and believe the Apostles' Creed, formulated at the end of the 3th century and accepted in the 4th century, as the theologians and clergy claim that it was inspired of the Holy Spirit, and that it summarizes the faith of the twelve apostles. Unfortunately, this is not at all right as there are no scripts evidencing this assertion. Ecclesiastics today do not realize that not even 10% of the Christians accept the idea of the resurrection of flesh, especially not when a person's body has been cremated.

We read many stories in the Bible about people who had been considered to be "dead" when they in fact had only lost consciousness. We read about Jesus raising people from the "dead" which does not necessarily mean that the person in question was clinically dead. Jesus raised from dead Lazarus for instance, as well as the son of a widow and he said about Jairus' daughter, whom people considered to be dead, that she was only sleeping.

"Now it happened, that he went into a city called Nain; and many of his disciples went with him, and a large crowd.

And when he came near the gate of the city, behold, a dead man was being carried out, the only son of his mother; and she was a widow. And a large crowd from the city was with her.

When the Lord saw her, he had compassion on her and said to her, 'Do not weep,'

Then he came and touched the open coffin, and those who carried him stood still. And he said, 'Young man, I say to you, arise.'

And he who was dead sat up and began to speak. And he presented him to his mother." (Luke 7:11–14)

Christian theologians reject the idea that Jesus was not clinically dead when they took him off the cross. They say, that if Jesus was not offered and did not die as the Lamb of God, then the central Christian dogma of Christ's saving the mankind is invalid and we are not redeemed. They also maintain that without Christ's resurrecting, we are not able to believe in eternal life. However, these are doubtful reasons, first of all because believing in the resurrection of the dead as well as in the life beyond has always been a part of all religions, including Judaism, so no crucifixion was needed to convince people concerning eternal life. Already before the crucifixion Jesus also talked about the Kingdom of Heaven and eternal life as well as about the descendance and ascendance of the human.

Jesus surviving the crucifixion and then his leaving Galilee is confirmed by different scripts. Even the authors of the gospels in the New Testament mention that the disciples were confused when Jesus talked about his departing.

The author of *The Secret Book of James* renders an interesting report of Jesus' appearing to a few disciples five hundred fifty days after the crucifixion.

"The twelve disciples were all sitting together, recalling what the Savior had said to each of them, whether in a hidden or an open manner, and organizing it in books. I was writing what is in my book. Look, the Savior appeared, after he had left us, while we were watching for him.

Five hundred fifty days after he rose from the dead, we said to him, 'Did you depart and leave us?'

Jesus said, No, but I shall return to the place from which I came. If you want to come with me, come.'

They all answered and said, 'If you order us, we'll come.'" (NH, The Secret Book of James 2,7 ... page 24)

This text suggests that Jesus was not dead and therefore the disciples were "watching for him". James' question "did you depart and leave us?" can be interpreted that Jesus stayed away from the disciples, maybe because of his bad physical condition after the crucifixion or because he feared the Jews who were searching for him.

We may also wonder what place Jesus referred to when saying "I shall return to the place from which I came." More than that, he invites the disciples to follow him to that place.

Did he invite the disciples to go with him to India or Tibet where he had been before the crucifixion?

The authors of the gospels resolve this puzzle by saying that Jesus ascended to heaven, but according to scripts circulating in India and Tibet, the Master continued his mission in Kashmir/Shrinagar teaching people until he became old.

Jesus' leaving Galilee and coming to India after the crucifixion is confirmed by Nicolas Notovitch (1890), author of *The Unknown Life of Jesus Christ,* as well as Swami Abhedananda and Nicholas Roerich, who were in Tibet and saw the very old documents reporting about Jesus' life in Asia. The lamas living in the Himis monastery who showed them very old scripts about Issa/Jesus, said that the Master left Galilee after crucifixion and came secretly to Kashmir/Shrinagar where he then lived surrounded by many disciples. It is said that two disciples, John and Thomas as well as Mary Magdalene followed with him to India.

It is known that Thomas really lived and died in India; it is also known that John lived in Asia and that in Kashmir/Shrinagar people visit the tomb of Jesus/Issa.

Actually, no special journey to Asia is needed to discover Jesus' connection with religions of the Far East. There are many characteristics in his doctrines and philosophy giving evidence of Asiatic influence. For instance, when Jesus said, *"I am the way ..."(John 14:6),* he used a symbol well-known in Taoism and Buddhism. **Tao, the Way** can be roughly described as the flow of the Universe, or as some essence or pattern behind the natural world that keeps the Universe balanced and ordered. Tao – the Way is considered to have ineffable qualities that cannot be defined or expressed in words but it has to be experienced and its principles has be followed or practiced.

Fish is a symbol connected to Jesus, Buddhism and other Asiatic religions. It symbolizes fearlessness, happiness and courage. Fishes swim spontaneously through the oceans freely and instinctively.

The Greek word for fish is *"ichthys"*. As early as the first century, Christians made an acrostic from this word: **I**esous **Ch**ristos **Th**eou **Y**ios **S**oter, i.e. Jesus Christ, Son of God, Savior.

Christian theologians of all the institutional denominations claim that the unauthorized scripts are wrong when rendering that the 33 years old Master survived the cross and later left Galilee for India where he kept on teaching until he became "old". However, there is one script whose validity the clergy should not doubt, and this is *Against Heresies,* written by bishop *Irenaeus* (died about 202) who actually reports about **Jesus' being "old"**.

"So, likewise, he was an old man ... Now, that the first stage of early life embraces thirty years, and that this extends onwards to the fortieth year, everyone will admit; but from the fortieth and fiftieth year a man begins to decline toward old age, which our Lord possessed while still fulfilled the office of a teacher ... those who were conversant in Asia with John, the disciple of the Lord, (affirming) that John conveyed to them that information ... Some of them, moreover, saw not only John, but the other apostles also, and heard the very same account from them, and bear testimony as to the validity of the statement." (Early Church Fathers; Irenaeus, Against Heresies, 2:22; 4–6)

"WHO HAS BEWITCHED YOU?"
(Galatians 3:1)

Paul, the apostle asks in a letter written to the Galatians:

"… Who has bewitched you that you should not obey the truth, before whose eyes Jesus Christ was clearly portrayed among you as crucified?

… … … … …

Are you so foolish? ***Having begun in the Spirit, are you now being made perfect by the flesh?"*** *(Galatians 3:1 … 3)*

Paul does not realize that it was he who started the "bewitching" by spreading his own gospel instead of the true message of Jesus. Unfortunately, the process of bewitching has persisted for two thousand years because many things that Jesus fought against, as hierarchy, conformity to rigid rules, hypocrisy, strange dogmas, carnality, have become characteristics of the Church of Christ.

Paul, a former Pharisee and persecutor of the followers of Jesus, did not tolerate any other teaching except his own when propagating his gospel among Jews and Gentiles. He writes to the Galatians:

"But even if we, or an angel from heaven, should preach any gospel to you other than what we have preached to you, let him be accursed." (Galatians 1:8)

There is evidence that Paul played different "roles" as a Christian leader; the books of the New Testament present him as a person who tries to preserve as much as possible of his former Jewish theological background by mixing the stories of Old Testament with stories about Jesus. However there are scripts confirming that Paul knew about Jesus' secret doctrines but he did not want to teach them publicly to everyone but only to a select few whom he considered to be spiritually mature to understand them. This information about Paul is rendered first of all by Valentinus, who was revered as a spiritual master and who almost became bishop of Rome (ca 140). Valentinus claims that he got this information from Theudas, a disciple of Paul who was initiated in those secret doctrines according to which the god whom most Christians worship as a Creator, God the Father, is in reality only the image of the true God. The creator people believe in is a *demiurgos (Greek), i.e. a lesser divine being.* It is not God the One, but the demiurg who reigns as king and lord, who acts as a military commander, who gives the law and judges those who violate it – in short, he is the "God of Israel".

Paul's different "roles" as a Christian leader is not totally surprising. He himself writes about his multiple "identities" in a letter addressed to the Corinthians:

"For though I am free from all men, I have made myself a servant to all, that I might win the more;

and to the Jews I became as a Jew, that I might win Jews; to those who are under the law, as under the law, that I might win those who are under the law; to those who are without law, as without law (not being without law towards God, but under law towards Christ), that I might win those who are without law;

to the weak I became as weak, that I might win the weak. I have become all things to all men, that I might by all means save some.

Now this I do for the gospel's sake, that I may be partaker of it with you." (1 Corinthians 9:19–23)

Paul worked hard when establishing Christian communities in different countries; he traveled a lot and even risked his life when fighting against authorities who wanted to stop him. However he did a big mistake when not choosing the true, original doctrines of Jesus. When he talked publicly and when he was organizing the first Christian communities, he turned back to his old Jewish faith mixing it with some new ideas. He seems to have missed Jesus' saying that *"No one puts a piece of unshrunk cloth on to an old garment; for the patch pulls away from the garment, and the tear is made worse.*

Nor do people put new wine into old wineskins, or else the wineskines are ruined. But they put new wine into new wineskins, and both are preserved." (Matthew 9:16–17)

As Paul and the later church fathers who were establishing the institutional church preferred to put "new wine", that is Jesus' doctrines into the "old wineskins" of Judaism, they ruined and bewitched Christianity from the beginning to the end. All the wars, hatred, schisms and other afflictions caused by Christian authorities during 2000 years could have been avoided if Paul and the church fathers had chosen Jesus' spiritual doctrines.

When Paul puts the ground for communities in different countries, he applies his former strict Pharisaic patriarchal view of men and women. We read in his letter written to the Corinthians:

"a man indeed ought not to cover his head, since he is the image and glory of God; but woman is the glory of man. For man is not from woman, but woman from man". (1 Corinthians 11:7–9)

He introduces strict rules concerning women's behavior in the Church. As women generally were not allowed to study or to have any social opinions or functions, he forbids women to talk in the churches. Paul wrote to his brethren in Corinth:

"Let your women keep silent in the churches, for they are not permitted to speak; but they are to be submissive, as the law also says. And if they want to learn something, let them ask their own husbands at home; for it is shameful for women to speak in church." (1 Corinthians 14:34–35)

When saying this, he pretends that he does not know anything about Jesus' women followers who were allowed to take part in the dialogues about God and to discuss the Masters' doctrines. He certainly knew that Mary of Magdala was considered by the disciples as the one whom the Master loved for her advanced spiritual character and wisdom. Paul does not mention about Mary in his scripts because, similarly Peter, he probably refused to accept Mary's outstanding spiritual character.

We read in *The Gospel of Mary* and other gnostic scripts about the conflict between Mary of Magdala and Peter who was not able to understand why Jesus let her know more mysteries than the other disciples got. Once he provoked Mary by asking her to recount any teaching the Master may have given her that the others did not know.

"Peter said to Mary, 'Sister, we know that the Savior loved you more than all other women. Tell us the words of the Savior that you remember, the things you know that we don't because we haven't heard them."

Mary tells them about the rise of the soul past the powers of Darkness, Ignorance, Desire, and Wrath, that keeps the soul from ascending. When Mary has finished, Andrew blames her because of the "strangeness" of her teaching, and Peter accuses her for lying about the Savior. When Mary cries, Levi defends her, saying to Peter: *'Peter, you have always been a wrathful person. Now I see you contending against the woman like the adversaries. For if the Savior made her worthy, who are you then for your part to reject her? Assuredly the Savior's knowledge of her is completely reliable. That is why he loved her more than us.*

Rather, we should be ashamed. We should clothe ourselves with the perfect human, acquire it for ourselves as he commanded us, and announce the good news, not laying down any other rule or law that differs from what the Savior said." (The Gospel of Mary with the Greek Gospel of Mary, The Disciples' Dispute over Mary's Teaching, 17,0/ The Nag Hammadi Scriptures, page 744)

Jesus' opinion about Mary as well as his answer to the disciples' question why he loved her more than the male disciples is marvelously rendered in *The Gospel of Philip*:

"The companion of the Master is Mary of Magdala. He loved her more than all the disciples, and he kissed her often on her mouth.

The other disciples ... said to him, 'Why do you love her more than all of us?

The Savior answered and said to them, 'Why don't I love you like her? If a blind person and one who can see are both in darkness, they are the same. When the light comes, one who can see will see the light, and the blind person will stay in darkness.'" (NH, The Gospel of Philip, 63,30 ..., page 171)

Even if Jesus used a parable when answering the disciples' question, they certainly understood that Mary was the person who saw the light, Jesus, the Son of Light and that the male disciples were the "blind" ones who were yet not able to understand who Jesus was.

Why did the Master kiss Mary on mouth has been a question discussed not only in the circle of the disciples but even by theologians and film producers today. It is surprising that the disciples did not know that kissing on the mouth was not a sexual act, but had a deeper, spiritual meaning in Jesus' interpretation. Jesus also kissed on the mouth his stepbrother, James when meeting him. James recounts: *"He kissed me on the mouth and embraced me, saying, 'My beloved! Look, I shall reveal to you what the heavens have not known, nor their rulers." (The Second Revelation of James, Nag Hammadi Scriptures, page 338)*

In my Hungarian family we used to kiss on the mouth family members when we met and when we departed.

Peter's depreciating attitude to Mary of Magdala has affected the church fathers' and later popes' opinion about her. In the sixth century Pope Gregory the Great went so far that he declared Mary to be a former prostitute. He did it in a sermon when he confused Mary of Magdala with the fallen woman, also called Mary, described in Chapter 7 in the Gospel of Luke.

Unfortunately, this image of Mary of Magdala has been later propagated in the Catholic Church as well as has inspired many artists painting her as a "prostitute."

The bewitchment of Christianity started in a quite early stage, already when the institutional Church was established. The representatives of this church became authorities who did not accept any other doctrines and church organization form except their own.

The bewitchment kept going on when the clergy of the institutional Church decided to include in the church even pagan religious traditions. Gentile symbols, for instance the pagan obelisk, which is even today a popular ornament outside Catholic churches, have been taken over.

The ancient Egyptians regarded the obelisks as symbols of the sun god Ra and placed them at the entrance to their temples.

The obelisk is also regarded in the occult as a phallic symbol. When it is erected inside a circle, it supposedly symbolizes the sex act. The Vatican obelisk in St. Peter's Square is erected within a circle, but this circle is considered to be a sun dial.

One Masonic writer, H.L. Haywood writes: "In some cases these crude rock pillars were thought to be the abodes of gods or demons, in others, homes of ghosts; and often as symbols of sex."

The obelisk standing in St. Peter's Square came from Heliopolis, Egypt where it was believed to have been built by Pharaoh Mencares in 1835 B. C. in honor of the sun. It was brought to Rome by Caligula in 37 B. C. and intended to be erected in the Vatican Circus.

In 1586, Pope Sixtus V had it moved to the center of St. Peter's Square, an enormous undertaking that required more than 900 workmen and 140 horses.

Many hundred church bells rang, cannon salutes thundered when Pope Sixtus celebrated Mass, read formulas of exorcism in order to drive out the bad spirits from the obelisk. After having been thoroughly "baptized", now it stands in St. Peter's Square of the Vatican as a symbol of the conquering power of the church. However, one should not forget, that for some "pagans", the obelisk was actually a solar symbol that represented a vital flow between heaven and earth, a way of communicating with the divine.

The bewitchment kept going on when popes and other clergy representatives did not heeded the Master's **"Put back your sword"** admonition and started wars in the name of God.

The first three hundred years were characterized by struggles and conflicts inside and outside "the body of Christ", that is the Church. The conflicts demanded the life of many Christian martyrs and heathens.

When Christianity after years of war and violence at last became an established religion in many Eastern and Western countries, a period of peace would have been desirable. But dark forces steered events towards more disruption. During the Middle Ages rivaling popes and patriarchs cursed each other and led Christ's Church to a schism establishing Eastern and Western Christianity in 1054.

The papal bull *"Ad extirpanda"*, issued by Pope Innocentius IV in 1252, helps us to understand how cruel the ecclesiastical policy of the Middle Ages was. According to the bull, all heretics who rejected the teachings of the pope and the rules of the Catholic Church should be "trampled to death like poison snakes." Incredible instruments and methods of torture were invented with the purpose to cause as much suffering as possible. The "Iron Maiden", for instance, was shaped like the body of a woman, equipped on the inside with sharp knives that cut the condemned victim's body to pieces. "Soli Deo Gloria" (To the glory of God alone) was the text written inside the instrument which was blessed and sprinkled with "holy" water by priests.

The cruel ecclesiastical policy of the Middle Ages did not only strike individual "heretics", in some cases it was even directed against entire groups of people. The Cathars, for instance, got into trouble because their belief was quite similar to Gnosticism. As in one of the many conflicts between the Cathars and the Catholic Church, a Papal Legate had been murdered, in 1208 troops were sent to take revenge for the murder. Abbot Arnold of Citeaux, who had been sent with the troops, reported:

"Our people did not take any consideration for social position, gender or age, we butchered almost twenty thousand persons and when the enemy had been ruthlessly defeated, the town was looted and burned down, so that God's vengeance was carried out in a marvelous way." (Quatation from Simonides'bok, *The Religions of the World*)

The "bewitchment" of Christ's Church was going on during Reformation too, when life-saving commandments like "You shall not kill" and "You shall love your neighbour like yourself" seem to have lost their validity.

Sir John Oldcastle, a follower of John Wycliffe, the great English reformer, was burned at the stake. Jan Hus, Czech theologian and reformer, who spread Wycliffe's ideas about ecclesiastic and social reforms on the Continent, met a similar fate. Books about ecclesiastical history do not contain exact particulars concerning the number of those who died in armed conflicts between Protestants and Catholics, but one can suspect that many had to pay with their lives, especially during the Counter-Reformation in Central Europe.

The two great reformers, Martin Luther and Jean Calvin, are not remembered as blameless ecclesiastics either. In 1525, during the Peasant Revolt in Germany, Martin Luther stood first on the side of the revolting peasants, but soon he changed sides, and, according to some sources, even asked for military intervention, with the result that the Peasant Revolt ended in a terrible bloodbath.

It is known that Jean Calvin, with exaggerated piety, forced strict, at times almost unbearable rules of conduct and religion on the inhabitants of Geneva.

"How could all this happen?" is a question which can be answered with Jesus' following words: *"light has come into the world,"* but **"men loved darkness rather than light**, *because their deeds were evil.*

For everyone practicing evil hates the light and does not come to the light, lest his deeds should be exposed. But he who does the truth comes to the light, that his deeds may be clearly seen, that they have been done in God." (John 3:19–21)

The time has come now that the truth comes to the light. We have to open our "bewitched" eyes and mind and repent all the mistakes committed
- against God, in whose name wars were started and people were tortured,
- against Jesus, who has been accused, tortured and misinterpreted,
- and against all Christians in the world who have been bereaved of the true knowledge about the One, The Supreme Being of the universe because scripts have been misinterpreted, destroyed or hidden.

A *new reformation of Christ's Church* is needed, this time on a deeper level, liberating Christianity from its old bewitched state. We have to put aside texts which:
- legitimate oppression,
- teach about a cruel and punishing God who wants to destroy his own creation at the end of times,
- set up religious and profane leaders from the Old Testament as examples to be followed despite of them having lived and acted like offenders of the Commandments;
- distort the truth about Jesus and his purpose on Earth, and
- threaten with a final apocalyptic at the "end of time", when the chosen ones will be saved and the others will be doomed.

According to The Gospel of John, Jesus used the parable of the good shepherd when he explained who he is and why he has come to our world:

"… *Most assuredly, I say to you, I am the door of the sheep.*

All who ever came before me are thieves and robbers, *but the sheep did not hear them.*

I am the door. If anyone enters by me, he will be saved, and will go in and out and find pasture.

The thief does not come except to steal, and to kill, and to destroy.

I have come that they may have life, and that they may have it more abundantly."

(John 10:7–10)

Christianity is bewitched because "thieves and robbers", that is powers and authorities wanted to humiliate Jesus from the beginning to the end of his life on Earth. The first "bewitchment" was the invention of the strange story we read every Christmas according to which he was born in a stable in Bethlehem in Judea surrounded by animals, a place which probable did not even exist at that time. The author's assertion that there was no other place for Mary but only the stable when she gave birth to her child, can be an insinuation that neither Jesus nor Mary deserved a better place than that. If we take into consideration that the chief priests, scribes and Pharisees called Jesus an illegitimate child and later a "deceiver" of the ancestor's tradition, the story of the rejected Mary and her child gets a new interpretation.

Powers and authorities depict a negative, humiliating image of Jesus not only by placing him in a stable, but even when they choose the most humiliating form of execution: crucifixion.

Unfortunately, the institutional church accepts all the humiliating stories about Jesus and rejects other information which presents a true, worthy and majestic image of him.

When putting together the missing jigsaws of Jesus' life, we find out that he probably was born in Betlehem in Galilee in a well situated family; he was very intelligent and studied not only in Galilee but abroad too; he wanted to reform not only Judaism which still had a lot of pagan elements in its rituals (offering animals for instance), but he also combated polytheism in Indian and perhaps even in Egypt.

He was chased and persecuted because of his new doctrines that contradicted the old teachings of the scribes and Pharisees. He was crucified, but he did not die on the cross. He was not the "Lamb" whom God had planned to offer in order to reconcile the sins of humankind. Jesus rejected the cult of offering animals or humans, so the Christian dogma of salvation by offering him on the cross, is absurd and not credible.

The contradictory images of Jesus do not affect only what Christians think of Christ, but also has a great impact on the image of God in whom people are supposed to believe. As the bewitched theologians and clergy teach about God of Israel as presented in the Bible, Christians are confronted with contradictions and absurdities that confuse them. They are supposed to believe in a god who
- likes offering animals, and before even man;
- acts like a king and is belligerent, punitive and prohibits men to get knowledge;
- does not want humans to ascend to eternal life, but wants to keep dead people in graves until the end of time when they will be arisen in "flesh body".

Jesus talks about a totally different Supreme Celestial Being according to the Nag Hammadi scriptures. He teaches about The One Pure Invisible Spirit, the power that generates Light, Love, Insight, Consciousness, Peace and Harmony.

The One
- has no chosen people but loves all nations,
- is not belligerent and
- does not want keep humans in unconsciousness and ignorance but wants to supply knowledge about the spiritual origin of Man.

"I WAS BLIND, BUT NOW I SEE"

While searching for the missing jigsaws of Christianity, I realized that A. Einstein was right when he asserted that we can never get knowledge about reality by only using abstract mathematical calculations and theories. If I apply his theory on faith, I would say that nobody can get faith only by reading "holy" books and scripts containing dogmas and theories written by theologians and clergy. I agree with A. Einstein that the personal experience is indispensable for discovering the visible and invisible reality.

Unfortunately, ecclesiastic authorities do not seem to agree with Einstein; they present dogmas and theological dissertations as the only way of attaining the true faith and turn down people's supernatural experiences as heresy. They do not take into consideration that Jesus never bothered writing dissertations and never claimed people to believe in dogmas. He talked to people in a simple way and did works that helped them to experience the supernatural.

People I met during my active years as a priest were not so much interested in discussing Christian dogmas; they wanted instead to talk about spirituality or about an inexplicable personal experience, for instance the apparition of the spirit of a deceased person or of an angel who helped them in a difficult situation.

Talking about angels generally and guardian angels particularly, has been an issue that has always engaged people all over the world. Paintings of celestial beings on the walls of graves in different countries suggest that celestial beings have visited humankind ever since prehistoric times. People in old times were probably as confused as we are in our time when supernatural phenomena occur. The difference is that in modern time, as we doubt everything that contradicts natural laws, we turn down appearances and experiences that we cannot explain scientifically.

Stories about angels and other celestial beings do not give final answers on all the great existential questions, but help us to put together the missing jigsaws of the visible and invisible reality, reminding us that *"There is something beyond the mountains, beyond the flowers and the song,/There is something beyond bright stars and the passion of my heart"* as the Swedish poet Dan Andersson writes.

The Old Testament renders stories about archangels, as Michael, Gabriel, Raphael and Uriel; all of them seem to be kind and helping angels. However, in the book of *Revelation* in the New Testament, we read about scaring angels who seem to serve a revengeful God.

People are most interested to talk about good guardian angels that intervene when they are asked to help people in need. Unfortunately, believing in angels and in supernatural phenomena was restricted by reformers, like Martin Luther and Jean Calvin for instance, who wanted the Christians to focus only on the Word, that is the Bible, and the dogmas of the clergy.

In spite of ecclesiastical decisions and scientific skepticism, people want to talk about their experiences, may it be the visit of an angel, a miraculous healing, near-death or out-of-body experience, and other kinds of supernatural phenomena. Inger Waern, who lives in Sweden, had at first not been sure that she should publicly talk about her experiencing angels, but then she decided to do more than that: she wrote a book, *Meeting Angels – Swedish recount,* reporting many people's angel revelation. In her book we read for instance the story of **Lena**:

"I want to tell you about a strange experience I had in my childhood. We were four or five children, aged five-six years, playing in my parents' potato cellar. We were sitting on the edge of the potato crates and hitting a table with some sticks we had collected in the forest. We made a lot of noise and had great fun. Suddenly we noticed that angels were standing behind us. We saw them clearly. Very frightened, we rushed

out and ran down the cellar slope while shouting: 'Angels, angels!' We rushed to mother and shouted that we had angels in the cellar. Mother thought we were imagining things and tried to calm us down, as we were very upset. When father came home from work, mother told him that we had seen angels in our cellar. Father went to check the condition of the cellar after our playing there. Imagine his surprise when seeing that the cellar had collapsed. Father and mother were very happy that the guardian angels had scared away us before the cellar collapsed!" (Inger Vaern, Meeting the Angels, page 35)

Another report is the touching story of **Elsa** who tells about angels giving her a sign when her mother died in a hospital: *"This happened in the late 'twenties. We were eight siblings; when I was twelve years old my mother fell ill and was taken to the nearest hospital. She was lying there and did not seem to get better. Father often went to see her in the hospital. I remember clearly that it was Monday. In the evening, almost at eight o'clock, when I was about to fall asleep, I suddenly became wide awake as I saw in a vision a host of angels flying up to the sky. I hoped that it was not a sign that my mother had passed away. About half an hour later we got a telephone message from father that mother had died at eight o'clock. … Mother had only been ill for ten days and was only forty-six years old. Father and we, children were in deep sorrow, but my seeing the angels flying up to sky, made me hope that she was escorted by all the angels I had seen." (Page 65)*

As all stories are based on subjective perceptions, partial descriptions and memory, we cannot check the validity of the events and of phenomena described. Generally, people telling their personally story, do not want to impose a particular spiritual worldview on the listener. They always hope that the stories speak for themselves. But, sometimes the stories provoke us to ask why only some people are miraculously healed and why only some people have apparitions of angels. We are never able to answer such questions but we may suppose that there is a reason in each event of our life. Several people who had experienced unwelcome, unexpected afflictions, realized later that those events were perfect catalysts for their changing lifestyle or view of life. Dr. Eben Alexander for instance, during his near-death experience, when actually his brain totally collapsed, got insight in other dimensions of the universe, an event that has totally changed his view of life. ***"I was blind, but now I see,"*** he writes in his book. *"My life now took on a new meaning as I understood just how blind to the full nature of the spiritual universe we are on earth – especially people like I had been, who had believed that matter was the core reality, and that all else – thought, consciousness, ideas, emotions, spirit- were simply productions of it." (Proof of Heaven, page 15)*

Jesus Christ's purpose was to cure our spiritual blindness by delivering knowledge about the mysteries of spheres of the universe. He said, *"I have come to eradicate their blindness, that I might tell everyone about God who is above all." (The Wisdom of Jesus Christ, BG 8502 121, 13)*

Jesus did not teach about leptons, protons and atoms, but about The Way to invisible eternal spheres as well as about The Eternal Light that is The Spirit existing in the spheres as well as inside and outside us, humans. The highest quality of the Spirit is Love, that cannot be measured with earthly instruments but only be experienced. Therefore he said to his disciples: *"A new commandment I give to you, that you love one another; as I have loved you, that you also love one another. By this all will know that you are my disciples, if you have love for one another." (John 13:34–35)*

LITERATURE AND SOURCES

Comment: Books in three languages, Hungarian, Swedish and English have been used as literature; the English translation of the titles is made by the author and is indicated in brackets.

HOLY BIBLE – New King James Version, published by Thomas Nelson Publishers 1982
Bibel 2000 – Verbum, Sweden
Balogh, Béla: A végsö valóság (The Ultimate Reality), Bioenergetic Kft., 2002
Zukav, Gary: Den dansande Wu-li mästarna (The Dancing Wo-Li Master) Askild & Kännefull
Paul Davis: Gud och den nya fysiken (God and the New Physics), Prisma, Stockholm, 1987
The Nag Hammadi Scriptures – Revised and Updated Translation of Sacred Gnostic Texts, edited by Marvin Meyer, HarperCollins edition, 2008
Pagels, Elaine: The Gnostic Gospels, Vintage Books – A Division of Tandom House, Inc. New York, 1989
JESUS – The Unauthorized Version / Ancient accounts of the unknown Christ, Profile Books, London, 2006
Ljungman, Ulrika: Padre Pio av Pietralcina, Artos&Norma, Sweden 2002
Pio atya világa (The World of Padre Pio) – translated and edited by Tekulics Judit, published in Budapest 2011
PIO atya levelei (Padre Pio's Letters to His Spiritual Director) translated by Krisztina Ménesiné Mezösi, Budapest, 2008

Madame Katharina Tangari: Történetek Pio Atyáról (Reports about Padre Pio), Etalon, Budapest, 2009

Don Gabriele Amorth: PIO ATYA, miként én ismertem (Padre Pio, as I knew him), publisher IHTYS, Oradea, Romanian, 2015

Morcaldi, Cleonice: Életem Pio atya közelében (My life near to Padre Pio), Etalon, Budapest, 2008

Hillerdal Gunnar/ Gustafsson Bengt: De såg och hörde Jesus (They saw and heard Jesus), Verbum, Sweden, 1973

Hillerdal, Gunnar: Så ger sig Gud till känna (God Reveals Himself), Proprins, Sweden, 1988

Dr Eben Alexander: Proof of Heaven / A Neurosurgeon's Journey into the Afterlife, published in Great Britain in 2012 by Piatkus

Eadie, Betty J.: Omsluten av Ljuset ("Embraced by Light" – google/internet), Forum, Sweden, 1995

Moody, Raymond A: Ljuset ur tunneln (The Life Beyond), Natur och Kultur, Stockholm, 1988

Raymond Moody: Reflections on Life After Life, 1975

Chopra, Deepak: Life After Death/ The Burden Proof, Dammförlaget, Malmö, Sweden, 2007

Waern, Inger: Möte med änglar – Svenskar berättar (Meeting Angels – Swedish recount), Libris, Örebro, Sweden, 1998

FATIMÁRÓL beszél Lucia nővér (Lucia, the Nun Recounts about Fatima) translated from Portugal and edited by P. Lajos Kondor SVD and Ince Ruttmayer OSB, Hungary

Millman, Dan & Childers, Doug; Bridge Between Worlds – Extraordinary Experiences That Changed Lives (Formerly titled *Divine Interventions*) HJ Kramer published in a joint venture with New World Library Novato, California, 2009

Dr Sartori, Penny: The Wisdom of Near-Death Experiences, Watkins Publishing, London, 2014

Apostolic Fathers – internet ; (Apostoliska fäderna, Verbum, Stockholm, 1992)

A Szentírás Magyarázata (Commentary on Bible), Budapest 1981

Calvin, Jean: Tanítás a keresztyén vallásra (The Institution of Christian Religion), Budapest, 1986

Cardier, Jean: Kálvin – Egy Ember Isten igájában (The Man God Mastered: A Brief Biography of John Calvin), Budapest, 1994

Stroebel, Lee: Fallet Jesus (The Case for Christ), Libris, Sweden, 2002

Tabor, James D.: Jesus Dynastin (The Jesus Dynasty – How to Explain Away the New Testament), Schibsted förlag, Sweden, 2007

Woodrow, Ralph Edward: Babylon misztériumvallása (Babylon Mystery Religions), Lantec Verlag, Germany 1992

Dr. Zakar, András: A sumér hitvilág és a Biblia (The Faith of Sumerians and the Bible), N.Y. USA, 1973

Kanaaneiska myter och legender (Canaanitic Myths and Legends translated to Swedish by Ola Wikander), publisher Wahlström&Widstrand, Sweden

Notovitch, Nicolas: The Unknown Life of Saint Issa/Jesus, source: google/internet

Swami Abhedananda: Kashmir O Tibbate, an account of his journey to India, Tibet, published 1929; source: google/internet

Roerich, Nicholas: Travel diary Altai-Himalaya, source: google/internet

Other internet sources:
- www.archaelogy.org/
- www.skeptically.org/scepticism/id11.html
- http://en.wikipedia.org/wiki/Miracle of the Sun
- www.padrepio.catholicwebservices.com: The Apparitions
- www.padrepio.catholicwebservices.com: Supernatural knowledge
- http://en.wikipedia.org/wiki/Tiberius Julius Abdes Pantera

Rate this book on our website!

www.novum-publishing.co.uk

The author

Eva Fogarasi Bálint was born 1952 in Transylvania (North-West Romania) where she belonged to the Hungarian minority. She left the country during the dictatorship of Ceausescu and settled down in Sweden where she studied Theology at the University of Lund. She was a priest in the Swedish Lutheran Church until she retired. She has written books in English, Swedish and Hungarian questioning the dogmas of the institutional church and pointing out the deficient information about Jesus and his teachings. The authorities of the Swedish Church accused her of deviating from traditional Christian theology and in January 2018, they suspended her from her role as clergy.

novum 🗨 PUBLISHER FOR NEW AUTHORS

The publisher

He who stops getting better stops being good.

This is the motto of novum publishing, and our focus is on finding new manuscripts, publishing them and offering long-term support to the authors.
Our publishing house was founded in 1997, and since then it has become THE expert for new authors and has won numerous awards.

Our editorial team will peruse each manuscript within a few weeks free of charge and without obligation.

You will find more information about
novum publishing and our books on the internet:

www.novum-publishing.co.uk